DANIEL

Joan Shapiro

A KISMET® Romance

METEOR PUBLISHING CORPORATION
Bensalem, Pennsylvania

First Printing June 1993.

ISBN: 1-56597-066-7

For Terey daly Ramin and Jeanne Savery Casstevens: where would I be without you guys? What a team we are: bullwhip, cattle prod, and cat-o'-nine-tails!

Special thanks to Norm Shapiro, RPh. and Dr. Larry Shapiro for their invaluable technical expertise and advice.

JOAN SHAPIRO

Joan has been writing for nine years—living proof that perseverance pays! From voracious reader to dedicated writer seems an obvious evolution and one for which she is forever grateful. Newly elected President of the Greater Detroit Romance Writers of America, in her spare time she's a part-time librarian and mother of three grown children: Bob, Larry, and Helene, who are now *True Believers*! She and Norm, her patient and proud husband, live just outside of Detroit, Michigan. Joan would love to hear from you at P.O. Box 521, Novi, MI 48376. (SASE, please).

ONE

"Where the hell is that damned pen?"

The denim-covered female bottom and the eloquent string of expletives brought a long-absent smile to Daniel Slayton's face. He stopped dead in his tracks, almost forgetting the blinding headache that had driven him into the small-town drugstore in the first place.

The subject of his speculations pushed herself, bare feet first, from under the display table in front of the prescription counter. Propelled by dusty hands, Edie levered herself to her knees, still muttering.

"Everything I touch turns to sh—"

Her words stopped abruptly at the sight of two expensively booted feet not more than six inches from her knees. Her gaze traveled up a long length of corduroy until it reached narrow hips, upon which rested a pair of large, well-kept hands.

Edie's visual journey skimmed the slight bulk of his stylish ski jacket. *Great-looking shoulders*. She tilted her head to see the face of the impressive specimen.

Impeccably cut dark hair was brushed back from silver-frosted temples, the perfect finishing touch. The almost square jaw was just saved from total granite angularity

7

by the mouth: the flickering smile gone, it was set now in a grim line, ravaged by pain and impatience. A straight nose led her to a forbidding frown and steady, cool gray eyes.

Piercing. Until now it was a description Edie had thought apt only in fiction. Wow!

She blinked and took a deep breath. This reaction was really stupid. *He's not the best-looking man I've ever seen. Give the devil his due—Mark was a pretty good hunk.* She blinked away the unwelcome image of her ex-husband and looked again at the man. Well, that's all he was, really. Just a man.

Right. And King Kong was just a monkey.

"I hate to interrupt but can I get this prescription filled?"

His sarcasm hit Edie like an ice cube down the neck. She blushed.

"Sorry. I didn't realize anyone was here." She tried a smile, her eyes crinkling with humor. "You walk so quietly you're either an Indian scout or the world's best cat burglar."

Well, for heaven's sake, she thought, *it was just a joke!*

Daniel's eyes narrowed, lips thin in annoyance. "The store is open. Do I need a blare of trumpets?" He reached for her elbow and hauled her unceremoniously to her feet.

It was about then the fuse of Edie's temper first began to sputter, though she made a valiant effort to tamp it down. "I'm sorry, sir." Her tone was civil, barely. "We close at four o'clock on Sunday." She looked pointedly at the clock, whose hands showed twenty-five minutes past that hour. Oh Lord, at this rate she'd never finish checking the stock.

"Well, then, it was careless to leave the door unlocked."

His tone set Edie's teeth on edge. She was *never* careless. Well . . . almost never.

Daniel took in her disheveled state, the mop of copper hair that looked as if she'd just taken an egg beater to it, the smudged nose, the disreputable clothing. And—good God, even the bag ladies on Detroit's Cass Corridor wore shoes!

Edie saw where his eyes were fixed but there was no convenient place to hide the offending feet. She began to edge toward the Rx counter, where she'd shed her shoes, when his next words stopped her in mid-slink.

"You haven't worked here very long, have you? Carelessness is usually the result of inexperience."

Edie's cheeks glowed pink and her words erupted without hesitation or thought. "There's a sign on the front door, *sir*, stating our business hours." *Damn, Edie, the customer is always right. Yeah, but does that count when he's pompous and rude?*

Suddenly the man's mouth distorted into an anguished grimace. He groaned and would have staggered but for the support of the counter. He rubbed his temples with such pressure the fingers showed white against the dark hair.

"Are you all right?" Edie's spurt of anger was forgotten in the face of his obvious pain.

"No," he said distinctly through set lips. "I'm not all right."

He ignored the hand she stretched toward him and looked to the prescription counter.

"Listen, I'm really in a hurry and I've wasted enough time already. Just be a good girl and get Mr. Mac, will you?" The rumpled figure of John McIlvain, the "Mr. Mac" of Mac's Drugs, was a long-familiar fixture in the town's one and only pharmacy.

Edie narrowed her eyes. *Good girl* indeed.

"You have a prescription?"

He massaged his temples and looked down at her

fixedly. "Of course I have a prescription." He looked
as if he wished her keeper would come and take her
into custody. "I'd like it filled . . . now, if you don't
mind."

He thrust the scribbled form at her, then jammed his
hands into the pockets of his trim gray down jacket and
stalked away to examine a fascinating display of contact
lens solution.

Daniel's anger now was directed at himself. Hell,
what was the matter with him? That was totally un-
called for. She'd done nothing to deserve that kind of
treatment. His temper, along with the rest of his emotions, was usually under better control. At least it used
to be.

Control. He'd had years to perfect the technique.
How had he lived a lifetime like that?

But in matters of survival one had no choice. And
control had been as necessary to survival in those early
years as air and water. Daniel had learned it, perfected
it—and now could not escape it. The incessant throbbing
behind his eyes, the awful pressure building inside his
skull told him that. Half a lifetime with total control,
and he foresaw the other half and no way to control it
at all. Agony sliced his skull and he lifted a shaking
hand to rub his eyes. Where the hell was Mr. Mac?

Edie read anger in the hard set of his shoulders and
the stiff gait of his long legs. What a miserable sour-
puss. And what a dirty trick: to waste a great bod like
that on the personality of a grinch.

She looked at the paper clutched in her hand. Daniel
Slayton. Obviously a tourist passing through. The Rx
blank was from a neurologist in Detroit. And despite
the carefully contrived informality of his clothing, there
was an aura of urbanity and sophistication about Mr.
Daniel Slayton that was out of place in a small town
like this. Anyway, there wasn't a soul she didn't know

and hadn't known all her life. She wouldn't have forgotten him.

She glanced again at his prescription. Good Lord, if he needed something this strong, he must be in real agony, and here she was wasting time ogling him. Galvanized by guilt she hurried into the back room.

It was only a few moments until the clicking keys of the ratchety old typewriter could be heard printing out the label. "At my age," Mr. Mac had growled at her when she'd asked, "I'll manage to do without these fool computers. Managed to get this far without 'em, guess I can go a little longer."

Now Edie glanced at the man over the top of the prescription counter. He rubbed his forehead again in an apparently futile effort to scrub away the pain, then turned from the shelf and moved aimlessly along the aisle.

Daniel was impatient to be on his way. If he hadn't promised George Corey at the community hospital that he'd stop to look at the plans for the new wing, he'd have been home long before the pain began burrowing its way through his skull. Perhaps there would have been no pain at all.

The antiseptic smell of the bright hospital corridors, the hushed, waiting atmosphere of the small surgery unit still unused at the moment but ready for the inevitable arrival of the first patient, the cabinets holding the dizzying variety of familiar instruments . . . he'd been away from it all so long. He pressed his fingers to the bridge of his nose. And not long enough.

But the meeting with Corey had been imperative. Construction was complete and the long-planned enlargement to the hospital's surgical area was ready to open. Daniel had consulted on its design and promised long ago to supervise the initial setup. After all, it had been his suggestion and donation that had begun the successful fund-raising, though it had taken no little

persuasion to convince Corey he was serious about re-
maining anonymous. This final meeting had been de-
layed too long.

It was, Daniel acknowledged, his own reluctance to
set foot in the building that had caused the delay. He
wondered now whether his qualms had been well
founded or if, ironically, they had become a self-fulfilling
prophecy, precipitating this latest attack. Whatever. Before the tan brick building had faded in his rearview
mirror the headache had taken a firm hold and wouldn't,
he knew, release its grip easily.

He wanted nothing so much as the welcoming darkness of his silent bedroom, the oblivion of sleep. For
a few hours, at least, he could escape the pain, the
memories, the emptiness within himself. But the pain
had been a reminder that he must have the necessary
medication at hand, always. Daniel walked to the open
end of the counter and looked down the length of the
raised platform behind it. His eyes widened. The only
person there was the sloppy young girl—and she was
filling his prescription.

"Stop that!"

His angry command startled Edie and she almost
dropped the small vial she was holding. Her head jerked
up in shock.

"Just what do you think you're doing? Where's Mr.
Mac?" Not in a million years, not under any conceiv-
able circumstances Daniel could imagine, would the elderly druggist allow an unlicensed clerk to dispense a
prescription.

Edie drew herself up to her full five feet three inches,
chin at a defiant angle. "Mr. Mac's not here and I'm
filling your prescription. That's what a pharmacist
does." The acid almost dropped from her lips.

"But," Daniel was, for a brief instant, speechless.
"But, you can't . . . you're just a kid."

He stared, bewildered. She was a cute little thing, in

a disreputable sort of way. Her softly rounded face was framed by chin-length hair the color of the autumn leaves drifting from the trees outside. It was tousled now as her hands pushed through it with careless disregard. The color of that hair should have been warning enough. "You can't be the pharmacist," he insisted again.

Slowly, thoughtfully, Edie peered at the framed certificate on the wall behind her. She studied it intently for a few seconds, as if memorizing its message. Then she looked at him over her sweatshirt-covered shoulder and nodded gravely.

"Well, I must be, don't you think? I mean, that's my name right there . . . Edith Stephanie Calvin." She enunciated each syllable slowly, clearly, as if he were particularly thickheaded and dull.

"Now listen, young woman—"

"Well, that's better than 'kid'!" she snapped, bringing his words to an abrupt halt.

Few people ever had that effect on Daniel.

Edie stood for a moment before she reached under the counter for her purse and pulled out a battered leather wallet. Opening it to the driver's license, she looked down at him and gestured at the photograph. "Yep, it's me, all right."

She was rewarded with the dull flush that colored Daniel's face. And her own immediate sense of remorse, which she tried to dismiss: he'd deserved it.

Well, Edie sweetie, you weren't such a pussycat, either. But, it's crazy, she thought. She always went out of her way to *avoid* antagonizing anyone; her big trouble had been the reverse. She didn't dish it out but she'd sure allowed herself to take it, far too long. She was still doing some damage control, even this long after the divorce. And now this total stranger had aroused a belligerent antagonism and gotten under her skin in a way not even Mark had—

Edie bit her lip. "Look, would you like an affidavit? How about a note from my mother?" Ah, what the hell, it was way too late to worry about alienating a paying customer. She hoped Mr. Mac would understand. Just so long as Mr. Daniel Slayton took his beautiful body and his ugly mood back out the door. Let him go wherever tourists went after passing through this wide space in the road on the way to Traverse City.

"What's wrong with Mr. Mac?"

"Nothing. He's fine."

"Where is he?"

Edie carefully finished applying the label to his prescription. Lord, it sounded like an accusation. "Don't worry, I haven't done away with him. He's alive and well and visiting his daughter in Atlanta for a couple of weeks. As long as I'm home for a while I'm minding the store."

She returned to the cash register, where Daniel stood silently waiting. He seemed to have lost his anger, looking slightly chastised by her not-so-subtle rebuke. Edie softened. She never had been comfortable on the battlefield when she could avoid it.

"I hope he gets a little rest," she continued the idle conversation. "It's the first vacation the poor man's had in years." Edie thought of the elderly pharmacist she'd known since childhood and her fond smile lent a subtle charm to her face.

Something there, the gentle humor, the tender concern, brought Daniel up sharp. He was suddenly very much aware of her, her quiet smile, her soft, full mouth.

What the hell was wrong with him? Five minutes ago he'd wanted to bite her head off.

He stared at her, and there was a curious expression in his silvery eyes.

Edie looked back at him, head tilted in an unspoken question. *Whoever said gray was a cold color?* The unbidden thought rattled her almost as much as his next words.

"I, uh, I'm . . . sorry I was so rude."

She could tell the mumbled words fit his mouth as awkwardly as her Aunt Essie's first set of false teeth. As unfamiliar, and just as uncomfortable.

"Well, I'm sorry too." She smiled hesitantly. "I don't know what came over me. Tired I guess."

Edie was beginning to feel the need for some armor. Too bad she'd discarded her white pharmacy jacket. He made her feel vulnerable, and that was one thing she couldn't cope with, not now, not so soon after Mark. She retreated behind the professional face and demeanor that always served her so well. "That will be seven eighty-five, please."

Daniel handed her the money and, at that instant, the frown line between his dark brows contracted into a deeper furrow, stamped there by a sudden, piercing needle of pain.

"May I have some water?" His face had gone ashen and his voice was unsteady.

Edie hurried to the sink and brought back a paper cup of water, her eyes warm with gentle concern. "Pretty bad, hmm?"

"It's been worse." His voice was weary and he looked at her from eyes filled with more pain and hopelessness than anyone ought to bear.

She had an impulse to reach out to him, touch—

Oh sure, *That* would give him a good laugh. She clasped her hands together on the counter. *I wonder if he knows how to laugh?* She tried to visualize it and failed.

Daniel fumbled with the childproof cap the law required and quickly swallowed the tablets, fighting to keep them down, almost nauseated by the relentless pain behind his eyes.

"There's a chair over here. Would you like to sit down?"

"No!" Daniel was angry with himself, with his surrender to the pain. The last thing he wanted was her pity. "I'm not an invalid, thank you!"

Edie gritted her teeth; she would not descend to sniping with him again.

"You know, you should be very careful with this medication. It would be a good idea not to drive too far tonight. Perhaps you can stay over—"

Daniel's evident irritation squelched the rest of her lecture.

"I know precisely what effect it will have. I realize you're fulfilling your *professional* requirements, but in this case I assure you it's not necessary."

Well, excu-u-u-se me. "As you wish." Edie was disappointed by the end of their too-brief truce. Ah, well, she wouldn't see him again once he left. And why didn't he?

Daniel turned away, already regretting his brusque words. The old resentment had popped up, like a reflex, as if on cue. And yet there was really nothing about her to remind him of Sandra. Carefully groomed, carefully unemotional, carefully professional Sandra.

At that moment the ancient Regulator clock on the back wall began to chime five o'clock, startling them with the reminder of evening's swift approach.

"Well," Edie murmured dryly, "time sure does fly. . . ." She didn't bother to finish the thought: *This had been almost as much fun as a toothache.* "Will there be anything else?"

"What?" Her voice brought Daniel back to the present. "Oh. No, nothing th—"

At that Edie smiled. She couldn't help it. He'd almost said it: *Thank you.*

And then of course he spoiled it.

"If you don't want any further interruptions, you'd better come and lock the door behind me."

It was his patronizing attitude more than the words. She'd put up with that too much in the past few years and she wasn't about to knuckle under to it now. As if she needed a keeper!

Daniel, by now a badly shaken Daniel, turned on his heel and started briskly for the door. He couldn't understand himself at all. He needed to get home. He needed to get away from *her*.

Irritated, Edie hurried after him, and at that point, events, having begun to unwind, took on a life and a momentum of their own—uncontrollable and unavoidable.

Intent on escape, Daniel never heard her quick footsteps closing in on him, a lapse that proved in retrospect to be very costly. He was totally unprepared for the final assault. His foot slipped on something lying on the floor and, thrown off balance, he tilted backward, into Edie coming up close behind. Arms flailing, she made a reckless grab for him, trying to regain her equilibrium.

Which she did. Unfortunately, he didn't.

Daniel found himself in a wild skid, propelled like a cannon shot, straight into a dangerous shampoo display lying in ambush. Bottles flew, along with a lot of other things, including a hapless Daniel Slayton. When at last he careened to a dead stop, he found himself wedged horizontally between scattered packages of pink hairnets and assorted sizes of pantyhose.

Like the inside of a giant paperweight, a snowstorm of suddenly liberated cottonballs floated lazily through the air. Edie watched, fascinated, as three of them settled in ridiculous puffs on his now rumpled and disordered hair. Two of the shampoo bottles seemed to have lost their caps and, as he stared blankly up into Edie's horrified face, the oh-so-proper Daniel James Slayton lll found himself sprawled on his back, awash in a spreading sticky green puddle of pine-scented foaming ooze.

Edie's lips twitched suspiciously.

"Don't." He gave the single word a sense of quiet menace.

She didn't.

But he looked so absurd, lying there, those ludicrous tufts of cotton sticking up on his head like molting feathers on a bedraggled chicken, surrounded by a mind-boggling mound of stocking-filled plastic eggs. Edie chewed her lip, tried desperately to restrain the laughter bubbling up in her throat.

Possibly ten very strained seconds passed and he lay there, eyes now closed, utterly still. And Edie was suddenly, frighteningly, faced with other, more fearsome possibilities.

"Mr. Slayton?" No answer. "Oh God, are you all right? I . . . I'm so sorry! I didn't mean to . . . I should have . . ." She babbled on, dropping to her knees beside him, trying to discover the extent of his injuries. She prayed things wouldn't get any worse.

Dear heaven, *could* they?

Edie ran her hands expertly up his legs, skimming the ribs of velvety corduroy, all the while murmuring a disjointed string of soothing words she hoped would keep him calm. Logic told her it would be about as effective as spraying Mt. Saint Helens with a garden hose. But logic—the rat—had deserted her sinking ship.

Her hands moved slowly . . . and stopped. Because, suddenly, she was aware of herself, and him, her hands and his body, and just exactly how intimately they were becoming acquainted. Cheeks hot, she forced herself to focus on his face.

The errant thought crossed her mind that his mouth was really sensational, even now. It had a strong masculine beauty, hard and sensual and exciting. Her busily exploring hands fluttered to a stop, resting for a dazzling moment at the indentation where his hip joined the length of muscular thigh.

They could put me away for what I'm thinking. Talk about assault and battery. I'm guilty of battery, and now I'm ready to assault. So where is all that cool professionalism, anyway? Her face a deep scarlet, she mustered as much bravado as she could and continued up the expanse of rib cage and chest that seemed to go on forever. His eyes, mercifully, were still closed.

"Mr. Slayton? Can you hear me?" Still nothing. "Oh please, *please* say something." She put a trembling hand on his damp forehead, trailing gentle fingers with a tender delicacy along his lean, pale face.

Daniel slowly opened his eyes to stare up at her in the sudden intense silence.

"Oh thank God! I, uh, I don't think you've broken anything."

"Are you quite positive you wouldn't like to go over it all again, just to make sure?" he mumbled with undisguised sarcasm.

She jerked her hands away and jumped to her feet. Asking him to speak was obviously another of today's mistakes! At that moment Edie knew precisely how a butterfly feels on the end of a pin.

Daniel held his body rigid, his expression blank, but he could do nothing about the long-atrophied emotions churning furiously, painfully. God, he hadn't thought he could feel that much, that quickly, not ever. It had been so long since he'd even cared. He'd had to grit his teeth to bite back an involuntary groan of frustration at the cloth separating his flushed skin from the touch of those soft hands.

She was so close he could feel every quick breath she took, see her shirt rise and fall with the movement.

So close. He felt like a prize idiot. She definitely was not the young girl he'd thought her. There was no mistaking the mature femininity of her face, and the loose sweatshirt and well-worn jeans couldn't completely disguise the curves beneath. They were enough to catch the attention of any man this side of the cemetery. And he wasn't that far gone. Not yet.

Daniel felt an unearthly warmth wherever her hands had lingered and, if he were honest with himself, he hadn't been ready for her to stop. Nerve endings were humming with the gentle stimulation of her fingers. He felt more alive than he'd felt in weeks . . . months. Years. And he found the throbbing in his head was muted to an almost bearable discomfort. The lady, he thought with self-mockery, had a very healing touch.

By now he was as red-faced as she, his breathing every bit as agitated. Escape. He needed to escape the growing discomfort of his arousal—and the cause, still crouched too close. Daniel braced his hands on the floor to lift himself upright . . . and came in contact with the forgotten object that had caused his calamitous slide.

Nervous, Edie watched him sit up, anticipating anger. She wouldn't be surprised if smoke poured from his shampoo-sudsy ears. He seemed to be foaming everywhere except the mouth. No doubt she wouldn't have to wait long for that charming spectacle.

But Daniel's initial impulse had paled into a kind of desperate fatalistic resignation. He held up the object that, quite literally, had been his downfall.

"What did I ever do to deserve you?" he muttered, then shook his head gingerly. "Forget it, I don't think I want to know." He glanced at his extended hand in dazed fascination. "At least we seem to have proved it beyond a doubt. It definitely is 'mightier than the sword.' "

Edie swallowed painfully, wishing the earth would open beneath her feet, her *stupid* feet, so she could find a place to hide. She couldn't tear her eyes from the offering in his hand.

He'd found her damned pen.

___ TWO ___

The single lamp burning in the living room cast long shadows into the hall as Edie let herself into the darkened house. "Lorraine! Hey, Lorraine, you miserable mutt, where are you?"

Silence. "Boy, can't even move her bones to see if it's friend or foe," Edie muttered. "Talk about lazy!"

She dropped her coat on the hall bench, almost overcome by exhaustion. Her legs ached, a pile driver had taken up residence inside her head, and the thought of bed held more allure at the moment than a slice of her mother's chocolate fudge cake. She grimaced, recalling the unholy mess she'd just cleaned up in the store. Industrial-strength tired.

In the kitchen, lit by the stove light, Edie spotted the note pinned to the refrigerator door by the pig-shaped magnet that warned of the dire connection between lips and hips. She grinned. "Stew in pot, pot in fridge, see you soon. Love, Mom."

Of course: Sunday night. Nothing short of fire, flood, or earthquake would stay her mother from the weekly meeting of the Ladies' Guild card game. The routine had been established more years ago than Edie could remember. It was as much a fixture in her life as these worn spots in the kitchen linoleum, or the third drawer from the top in her dresser that stuck, or the temperamental shower spray that was, at its own unpredictable whim, likely to scald or freeze you without warning.

She closed her eyes tightly and ran her fingers lovingly over the chipped Formica counter surface. God, how she loved it, this old house, with all its quirks, its drafts, its antiquated plumbing. She hadn't realized how she missed it, all those years she'd been gone. True, it didn't have the newest decorator's touch and it lacked an aerie-level panoramic view, marble floors, and giant TV screen. But it had one thing that her recently vacated Chicago lakeshore condominium had never had: every corner was filled with happy memories.

Well. She rubbed her moist eyes with the back of a hand and took a deep, steadying breath. "Stop dawdling, Edith—tempis is fugiting." She transferred the stew to the oven, set the temperature on low, and made her way up the dark stairs to her bedroom. While she undressed, Edie looked fondly at the cheerful clutter of the room she'd called home for most of her life.

From toddler to teen these walls had sheltered her, been privy to pajama parties and temper tantrums, witnessed her heartbreak when she failed to make the cheerleading squad and her triumph when she landed a small part in the senior play. Here she'd found refuge when Jimmy Dahlgren (oh be still, my teenage heart!) asked her best friend Annette to the prom. And Annette accepted! Edie had thought she'd "just die." And now, she grinned, she could hardly remember what he'd looked like. Jimmy *who*?

A good lesson, that. Nothing lasts forever, not pain and not love. *Not love*. Oh, ain't it the truth! From Jimmy through Mark, she'd fooled herself about love for the last time. *The head will rule the heart next time, you ninny*. Since her first pair of high-top shoes, Mom had been telling her: *Watch where you're going, sweetie.* But did she listen? Why had she needed Mark to finally learn what a loving mother would have taught her without all the pain?

With a tired gesture she rubbed her eyes. Enough! Mark would stay in the past, where ex-husbands belonged; he was not going to invade this part of her life with his special brand of torture. Edie dumped her thoughts, along with her underwear, into the hamper with the rest of the dirty laundry and climbed into the shower.

Mmmm! Empty plate pushed aside, the last of the diet pop swallowed, Edie folded down the page of the almost-finished paperback novel. She leaned back at the scarred wooden table that had held so many meals in the big old kitchen, stretched, yawned. Right now the only problem her mother's beef stew couldn't cure might be a bad case of dandruff, and she wouldn't bet on it.

It was an incredibly short mental leap from dandruff to shampoo. And Daniel Slayton.

A wry smile stretched her lips. The psychologists were indeed right; there was definitely something to free association. Just look at him, hiding there in her mind all this time, waiting for the first chance to jump out and take over. She might have known he'd be impossible to control. What was there about the man that took hold of her, like a burr clinging to the edge of a sweater?

He wasn't exactly handsome, though he was handsome enough. And his body wasn't really that spectacular, though her fingers had proved it was spectacular enough! The corner of her mouth twitched as she recalled his trim physique. Nice set of buns, too. But, unlike some blind dates she'd had, he'd failed to demonstrate an "interesting personality," much less the requisite "great sense of humor." Great? Poor Daniel Slayton, unless you counted "bad" he didn't have any humor at all.

Poor Daniel Slayton. And yet, he was not a man to inspire sympathy—except perhaps for those first awful moments he lay there on the floor, looking so absurd, like a molting chicken. She felt an irresistible urge to giggle.

In the midst of her laughing reminiscence the click of the back door announced the arrival of Lillian Calvin.

"Hi, sweetie, what's so funny? Mmm, that stew smells wonderful, if I do say so myself. What time did you finally get home? Oh, did you give Lorraine her snack? We're all out of ice cream, except that diet stuff, and you know she doesn't like—"

"Mother, take a breath, for heaven's sake!" Edie was laughing now with genuine affection. Her mother had that kind of effect on people, even her only child. It was akin to being caught in a tornado and having your breath sucked away: it left you gasping.

"Oh, sorry, dear." Lillian smiled serenely. She herself was never flustered in the face of anyone else's confusion. She was the calm eye of that tornado, forever unruffled.

Lillian daintily dipped two fingers into the cooling pot and popped a chunk of meat into her mouth, unabashedly enjoying the taste of her own cooking. "So," she mumbled between swallows, "you were laughing when I came in—tell me what's so funny. I could use a good laugh. Would you believe I lost every hand tonight? My entire budget is shot!"

"You lost the whole two dollars?" Edie grinned. Sweet, unassuming Lillian's resemblance to a Mississippi gambler was legend and her losses were so infrequent as to be almost nonexistent. In her intimate circle of friends she wasn't called Jaws for nothing. "Well, the pros in Las Vegas might be ashamed of you, but the other sharks in the Ladies' Guild will have happy memories of tonight, that's for sure.''

"Don't be nasty, Edith Stephanie." That was her name when Lillian was annoyed. She hung her heavy coat on the hook next to the door and began to heat water for tea. "You don't have to rub it in. Anyone can have an off day, you know," she admonished her daughter in an injured tone.

"Oh yes, I know. Believe me, I know. Today was definitely one of mine."

"That bad, huh? You look tired. Must have been very busy for a Sunday. So, what were you laughing about when I came in?"

"Well, it really *was* funny, in a twisted kind of way. . . ." Edie told her mother what had happened, describing it in detail, with some well-chosen omissions, as they sat companionably at the table.

"I'm glad I don't have to face the poor man again. I'd either pass out from embarrassment or laugh in his face." *Or maybe tear his clothes off.*

"A tourist, hmm? How does he know Mr. Mac?"

Edie stared at her mother for a moment. "Gee, that's funny, I never thought to ask." She shrugged, dismissing the question. "I guess he's come through here before."

"What was his name again, dear?" Lillian asked absently before she swallowed the last of her tea.

Oh so casual, Edie deliberated, as if trying to remember an unimportant detail. "Uhm . . . oh, Slayton, I think. Yes, that's it, Daniel Slayton."

"Oh!" Lillian's eyes widened and the corners of her mouth turned up in recognition of the name. Edie felt more than just a faint stirring of curiosity. She waited expectantly while Lillian pulled a plate of cranberry muffins from the back of the counter, then poured another cup of tea.

At last Edie lost the battle to control her impatience.

"Well, what about him?" The words burst from her lips with more force than she'd intended.

"Hmm? Oh well, dear, he keeps to himself most of the time but he's always been very nice, quite pleasant to everyone." She dunked a piece of the muffin into the cup, then plopped the soggy blob into her mouth, chewing absently, her thoughts back at the card table, mulling over her ignominious defeat.

Always?

"Mother, do you *know* him?" Uneasiness spread rapidly as the germ of suspicion grew, flowering inside to a full-grown sense of dread.

"Of course, dear. He owns the old Gallatin place, on the south shore of the lake. You remember it, don't you? Such a shame they had to sell, but of course, with their boys living out west and—"

"Mother, please!" Edie didn't need to be regaled on the wanderlust of the Gallatin brothers. "How long have you known this . . . uh, Mr. Slayton? When did he move here?"

"Well, now, let me see. Annie and Richard's twins are eight, and Aunt Essie had her gallbladder out the next year . . . yes, seven years ago last June. They used to come up in the summer."

They?

"But after a couple of years she didn't come anymore."

She.

"Umm, uh, so, what's his family like?" Edie mumbled in an elaborate show of unconcern. *Why had she asked? Who cared?*

Guess who?

"Well, he comes up alone now. I remember hearing once . . . was it Sam over at the post office? . . . anyway, I heard he wasn't wearing a wedding ring anymore."

Boy, oh, boy, Edie shook her head smiling, *they didn't miss much in this town.*

"He's stayed on later this year, no one knows why. Never did see any children. Too bad, too, he's such a nice, charming man." Lillian prided herself on her character judgment, based on little intangibles no one else considered worthy of notice. Her record of accuracy was enviable, but this time her radar had apparently malfunctioned.

"Wait a minute," Edie interrupted, "we're not talking about the same person. That is *not* the man I met." Not that man with the angry laser eyes and the glacial voice.

"Darling, you did say he was in terrible pain. And, knowing you, I imagine you might have offered a little provocation, hmm?" Lillian raised her eyebrows expressively at her daughter. "Really, dear, flat on his back on the drugstore floor, how would you expect him to act under the circumstances?"

Edie squirmed. Even beneath his bad humor and pain she'd sensed . . . something, some fleeting glimpse of warmth, at least the grace to be ashamed of his bad manners, and that surprising hint of confusion at her concern for him. As if he were genuinely mystified by sympathy. Goodness, did money and humanity always have to be mutually exclusive? What sort of people was he used to, anyway?

A cynical expression twisted her mouth. She could well imagine. Six years of Mark had introduced her to some of them—plastic people who smiled at you but not *at* you, who talked but didn't listen, and for whom faith, hope, and charity had been replaced by Dun and Bradstreet. Edie shivered, overcome with a surprising surge of tenderness for Daniel Slayton. She'd gotten away from them without permanent damage to her psyche, but it had been a close call. Obviously he hadn't been so fortunate.

But she had to admire the restraint he'd clamped on his anger. He'd returned her pen, slowly freed himself from his sticky bonds and the miscellaneous debris, and managed a scruffy yet strangely dignified retreat into the cold October darkness. She chuckled now, recalling his transformation at her hands—*Gentleman's Quarterly* to Skid Row, in one easy lesson! A "little provocation"? *Mother knows best.*

"I don't know, Mom. It was more than that, more than physical pain—" Edie stopped abruptly before she said anything further. Lillian didn't miss much either.

Edie shrugged. "Well, no matter. It's not up to me to psychoanalyze every patient who brings in a prescription to be filled. I'd better ignore the mind and stick to the body."

A blush stained her cheeks when she recalled the examination she'd given that particular body while he lay on the floor at her mercy. She hadn't meant to cover quite so much territory quite so thoroughly.

She felt all over again the delicious warmth that spread through her when she moved her hands over Daniel's chest and shoulders. The heat of his body burned through the soft cashmere and, beneath the heavy corded fabric, his legs had been solid and muscular, the legs of a man in very good condition. The rest of him seemed to be in very good condition, too!

Her heart thumped crazily in the too-tight confines of her chest and her body reacted, now as it had then, as if she'd put her finger into an electrical socket. She'd had to fight to break that contact: it was eerie . . . and marvelously exhilarating and tough to hide behind feigned disinterest.

Abruptly Edie pushed herself from the table. "Well, time to hit the sack, I guess." This man, this stranger—an unpleasant man, a man she didn't even like—had taken up entirely too much of her time.

No, that was unfair. He'd been unpleasant, but he'd

also seemed . . . very lonely. The sudden insight surprised her.

Lillian rose too, yawning, and kissed Edie on the cheek. "I'll see you in the morning, dear. Try to get a good night's sleep. You look a little peaked."

Peaked. Edie smiled and suddenly hugged her mother tightly. She hadn't heard that word in years. "Go on, Mom, I'll just clean up these things before I come up." She turned to the sink, stepping automatically over the heap of wrinkled brown and white fur lying in disarray next to her chair.

"Well, well, the elusive Lorraine. Hello, you lazy thing. When did you come in, you intrepid old watchdog, you!"

Edie deposited silverware in the sink, then knelt down beside the shapeless mass. A wrinkled sad-faced basset hound face peered out from the knobbly pile, her expression permanently frozen into a state of mournful, martyred unhappiness. Edie nuzzled the dog's floppy left ear and rubbed lovingly along the neck and back of her sorrowful-looking companion. Lorraine's look of patient acceptance of life's indignities was a startling reminder of Daniel's face as he'd looked when she last saw him, and Edie burst out laughing at the absurdity of the thought. Man and dog, soul mates under the skin. She thought the comparison might be a disservice to the dog.

Lillian, halfway out the door, swung around at Edie's sudden outburst. "Darling, what in the world . . . ? What's the matter with you? Did Lorraine do something?"

"No, Mom," Edie grinned, "she didn't do anything. She just looks so . . . so . . ." She made a small choking sound. "That's how Slayton looked at me when . . . well, it just struck me kind of funny." She looked at the dog's reproachful expression, then up at her mother's still uncomprehending stare.

"I guess you had to . . . be there," Edie gulped, biting her lips and wiping her eyes. She rose to finish her chores.

"Yes, dear, of course."

Lillian's thoughtful gaze rested on her daughter for a moment more, noticing a few things Edie herself was not aware of—the eager animation in her voice, the new sparkle in her eyes, the slight blush. It had been so long since this vibrant, excited Edie had been around. But now, something, or *someone*, had brought her back again.

On her infrequent visits home over the past few years, the face Edie had shown, while still loving, was subdued, weighed down with the intangible burdens she held inside, reluctant to share with anyone. With masterful restraint Lillian had refrained from voicing the questions and doubts in her mind.

By then, of course, she'd known there was trouble in her daughter's marriage but she was too wise a woman to disturb, even from love, the delicate balance Edie struggled to maintain. Lillian respected her wishes and her privacy. But her heart ached for the happy face she'd once known, the joyous laughter in the soft amber eyes, the way the young Edie had rushed out to meet life head on, so sure she would find only wonderful things ahead of her.

Now her child was laughing again, a healthy, cleansing laughter this house hadn't heard in too many years. And, it seemed, Daniel Slayton was responsible. Interesting. Very interesting.

The muffled sounds of night filtered through the windows of the darkened room. Daniel lay atop the spread, inert, arms heavy at his sides, anticipating patiently the final phase of this latest battle with a familiar enemy. He waited for healing sleep to complete the job begun by the medication, but the thoughts forcing themselves to the surface gave him no rest.

The image of soft, warm, golden eyes glowed in his memory, a beacon promising some wondrous surprise. There was such a natural vitality, a sense of joy and life, and he had wanted it badly—wanted her. For that brief moment when she knelt by him, and then moved those smooth, steady hands over his body, he'd felt the beginning of something he hadn't known for . . . how long had it been since he'd felt interest or excitement or desire, for anything? Too long to remember. Long enough to be unprepared.

It didn't seem possible. The ultimate pragmatist— that's what he was, what he'd always been, what he'd been groomed to be, and he'd prided himself on it. And he'd been struck dumb by a sloppy, tart-tongued, bristly little country girl . . . with lovely copper-colored hair and golden eyes, eyes that shone with concern and understanding. Her mouth was soft, sweet with promise, and her small, firm hands left a heated trail behind them, burning into his skin with such force that even now, hours after that casual encounter, he still could not erase her from his mind.

Her face formed once more in the chaos of his thoughts, bringing with it an ineffable calm, a peaceful drift of serenity. As he sunk farther into the soft cocoon of sleep, his last thought was . . . her.

Interesting, he mused drowsily. Very interesting.

THREE

The drugstore, Edie reflected with some satisfaction as she locked the door behind her at six o'clock that Monday evening, ranked just behind Helen's Klassy Kurl and a little ahead of the grocery when it came to attracting gossip-hungry citizens. They came like bees to the honey, and the bees had been buzzing as usual today. Enquiring minds want to know!

Funny, though, she mused, cautiously easing her little Mustang into the street, since she'd been back no one had ever mentioned Daniel Slayton. He seemed to have blended into the background with all the ease of a seedling in the forest, and that was more than a little surprising. Everyone knew, *and* discussed, everything about everyone, and newcomers were the juiciest grist for the local gossip mill. A mere seven years made Slayton a newcomer.

Edie wondered, for an instant, why she hadn't run into him before. That was surprising, considering the insular nature of the community. Unless he were deliberately avoiding contact with those "enquiring minds." At the very least she'd have expected a good deal of speculation about the elusive Mr. S.: his health, his income, his favorite food, even his favored brand of underwear. Brand X from the supermarket would have placed him squarely among the majority.

But no one seemed to know a blessed thing. The man didn't even have the decency to hire a local woman to come in and clean house for him, for heaven's sake. He'd gone and hired a service from over in Beulah!

This is really dumb, Calvin. Why should you care?

She'd have been surprised how easily her mother could have answered that question.

Oops! She'd almost forgotten the ice cream! With hardly a moment's hesitation she jerked the wheel of the car and swerved around into an abrupt U-turn. Heaven forbid Lorraine should go two nights in a row without dessert. She pulled up to the grocery store and hurried in.

"Hi, Sarah." On her dash back to the frozen food section Edie waved to the young woman behind the cash register. Sarah smiled and waved back, then continued unpacking a carton of candy bars. She'd been two years behind Edie in high school, so they hadn't been close. But since Edie's return they'd resumed their acquaintance and the difference in years had vanished.

Edie set down the two half-gallons of French vanilla and handed her money across the counter. "I'm sure glad you're still open. Come to think of it, *why* are you? Go home!"

"Yeah, yeah, I know," Sarah agreed. "Stan just phoned. I'll be finished by the time he picks me up." She leaned on the counter and smiled as Edie read the T-top stretched across Sarah's burgeoning middle: "Incubator," beneath the sketch of an egg and an arrow pointing straight down.

"Close, hmm? How're you feeling, Sar?"

The younger woman pushed her hands into her sides, splaying the fingers across her back to ease the constant pressure, and blew a stray blond curl out of her eyes.

She looks tired, Edie thought, *but she's positively glowing*. She throttled the quick stab of envy.

"Oh, these last two months . . . it's forever. I am so *sick* of maternity clothes!" Sarah grinned, the joy on her face belying the complaint in her words.

"Stan's going to miss the hours you've been putting in here, I'll bet. What'll he do without you?"

Stan and Sarah had married within two years of their graduation and three years ago finally saved enough to buy the small store. With time and hard work they had managed to reach a comfortable state of semi-solvency.

"He's got Chuck Oleson and Pat Caskie part time. They'd love more hours, so it all works out fine. *They'll* be prosperous, *I'll* be retired, and Kevin and Brian will be thrilled to have their mother around as a full-time audience. And they've already informed me they want another boy, no 'dumb, sissy girls,' " Sarah chuckled.

"Why those little chauvinists!" Edie grinned back. "Just by being born this kid's gonna make so many people happy."

"Especially Stan! Poor man, he hugs me good night in stages. I started calling him Captain Cook, 'cause every time he holds me he has to work his way around the globe." They both burst out laughing and she ruefully indicated her exploding waistline. "Lord, remember when I actually had hipbones?"

Edie pocketed her change and gathered up the bag. "Listen, kiddo, I don't even remember when *I* had hipbones. Oh well, it's all chocolate syrup under the bridge," she grinned. "Guess I'd better head for home before Lorraine gets withdrawal symptoms. Poor old thing, she doesn't have hipbones anymore, either." Edie made a face at the bag and Sarah grinned back. Lorraine's idiosyncrasies were well known.

Edie hurried out to the car and stowed her precious cargo beside her on the seat. She sat for a moment, smile fading, the key held motionless in her cold hand.

Stan and Sarah. The conversation had been a sharp reminder that Sarah, although two years younger, already had two children at home and was almost at number three. It was not a thought Edie chose to dwell on.

There'd been a time when she'd desperately wanted a baby, hers and Mark's, but they'd faced repeated disappointments. Well, she thought wryly, at least *she'd* been disappointed. Later, of course, she realized he wasn't. It turned out to be just as well Mark had been denied what, for him, would have been the dubious joys of fatherhood. He'd have handled it as badly as he'd handled marriage. She took a deep breath. Pretty badly.

Ah, the hell with you, Mark Killian, M.D., S.O.B.

Angry with her rehash of unwelcome memory, Edie turned on the ignition, shifted into reverse, stomped on the accelerator, and—

"Oh damn!"

The sudden jolt, an ominous crunch of metal and breaking glass, told her she'd made a major miscalculation. Turning off the engine, she closed her eyes, resolutely straightened her spine, and opened the door. The slam of the other car's door was followed immediately by the garbled threats of the driver, directed at "the jackass" who'd just attacked his innocent car.

Edie made out the sleek lines of a black and silver Jaguar. *What a beauty*, she thought enviously, or at least it had been. At present it was quite unmovable. Shoot, she could take full credit for that: she'd just demolished its right front fender. It was crumpled like a used and discarded piece of foil, its edge pushed so completely into the tire the car couldn't be driven at all. In the spill of light from the store window it was a few seconds before the other driver's features became recognizable.

"Oh damn" was right! In such a small town it was inevitable she'd run into him sooner or later. Now she

had—ho, ho, ho—and wished devoutly it had been much, much later. Because she was dead meat. Definitely dead. If she were lucky, he'd bury her quickly.

She sure didn't feel lucky.

And now she'd never find out if he could smile—*because he was going to kill her first.*

Daniel Slayton, hands balled into fists, stood staring at the indignity she'd inflicted on his car. Abruptly, he turned on her. "Why the hell didn't you look . . ." His voice trailed off in astonishment and his eyes widened with recognition.

He'd known he'd see her again, he just hadn't expected it to be so soon. Indeed, if he could, he'd have avoided her altogether, although in a town this size that was less than probable. He couldn't imagine how he'd managed it so far. Now, in the indirect glow of the storefront lights, her face was ashen, afraid, and unsure. She stared at him in shock and fear at the realization of what she'd done, and to whom. Again.

For a moment Daniel had the bizarre impulse to apologize for somehow upsetting her. God, it was happening again! He was a rational man but this, whatever *this* was, was totally irrational.

For a moment *he* was afraid.

He forced himself to concentrate on the car. He tore his eyes from hers, and scanning the twisted mass of metal, Daniel was profoundly grateful for the flash of annoyance that blotted out the image of her face. He grabbed his anger and held it, hid behind its protective shield while he regrouped. He inhaled deeply.

"Okay. Now that you've got my attention . . ."

His sarcasm was interrupted by her small groan. It might have gained his sympathy in any other circumstances. His foot crunched on the broken glass of the headlight, a forcible reminder to eliminate sympathy from his repertoire.

"Look," he ground out harshly, "will you please

explain just what it is about me that sets off these strange attacks? I *assume* it's only me. Otherwise they wouldn't let you run around loose.''

"I . . . I'm terribly sorry, Mr. Slayton," she muttered.

"You're sorry." He clenched his jaw and ground his teeth at the same time.

Edie watched, fascinated. She'd never seen anyone do that. Wisely she refrained from commenting on it. "Look, I—I know it was my fault, but my insurance will cover it," she rushed on, her voice now a strangled whisper, "no matter what it costs." Jeez, a Jaguar. It would cost.

Edie brightened for an instant, a sickly smile struggling to life. "Say, maybe it's not as bad as it looks." She looked at it, then him, hopefully.

"God protect me from optimists," Daniel growled, "you and your eternally half-filled glasses."

"Well, it's better than always complaining they're half empty," she mumbled. She could carry this meek and apologetic business just so far.

"I *never* complain, and I—"

He stopped abruptly, startled to find himself standing in the middle of the street ready to exchange insults with her like unruly, brawling children. How quickly his restraint had vanished. Edie, opening her mouth for an equally quick retort, closed it almost at once. It seemed to occur to both of them in that instant how ridiculous their behavior was.

"Look, Mr. Slayton," Edie took a deep breath, wanting to placate him. She was, after all, though it galled her to admit it, the guilty party. "I know I should have looked first. I was thinking of . . . of something else," she finished lamely, recalling her thoughts of Mark. *Thanks a lot, Mark. Another fine mess you've gotten me into.* If his neck had been within reach, she'd have gladly put her hands around it and squeezed.

"Well, I'll never be able to drive this home." Daniel cast an accusing look at Edie and her undamaged car. "*Your* car's all right!" They both peered at it. At least they could agree on something.

"Okay," he said with decision. "You'll drive me to the gas station so I can get this towed off the street. Then you can take me home."

Satisfied, he dusted off his hands and headed for her car, not waiting for a reply, supremely confident he could take her agreement for granted. Edie's temper flared at his autocratic manner, but he didn't see the expression on her face and, wisely, she kept her mouth shut—because at that moment she heard the unwelcome sound of tearing fabric. She stared at him, eyes fixed on the leg of his khaki pants, ripped across from front to back, caught on the jagged metal of the fender as he walked past.

Oh Lord, this night will never end, Edie thought wildly.

Daniel stood, frozen in place, staring helplessly at the shredded fabric where a perfectly good pants leg used to be. Somebody up there really had it in for him! Lips compressed tightly to keep his thoughts unspoken, he got into her car, slamming his door. The noise echoed loudly in the night's stillness. If he needed an antidote for the tenderness she'd aroused in him, she seemed hell-bent on supplying it.

Edie slid into her seat and closed the door with exaggerated care. He sat beside her, arms folded across his chest, jaw rigid, eyes staring straight ahead. She knew she was in the presence of a man with one overriding concern—the prevention of a murder. Hers. They sat waiting, and finally he spoke, the words enunciated with care and precision.

"How long must we sit here? You can't possibly enjoy my company this much." The implication was clear that the feeling was completely mutual.

"I can't back up," she mumbled. "Your . . . car is . . . uhm, in the way."

He closed his eyes, took a very deep breath. "I see."

With exaggerated care he opened the door and, after a moment's pause, got out and went back to the disabled car. After putting it in neutral, Daniel managed to rock and push the Jaguar back far enough for Edie to maneuver past it and escape the parking space. They drove off, leaving his wounded beast crouched amid the debris in the street, its emergency blinkers like two agitated red eyes, flickering reproachfully in the dark.

It didn't take long for Daniel to make arrangements at the gas station, and by the time Edie was headed toward the lake to take him home, the tension in the car finally began to ease.

"I see you don't need directions."

The sudden sound of his voice, cool and distant in the semidarkness of the car's warm interior, startled her. It was, she thought, the first time he'd spoken to her without insults or anger. It was an unexpected surprise. The low timbre of his voice crawled suggestively up her spine, and she felt a shiver all the way down to her fingertips clenched around the wheel.

"How did you manage to find out where I live?"

"I didn't *manage* it." He needn't think she was interested enough to ask! "I . . . happened to mention your visit to the store yesterday when I was talking with my mother, and she recognized your name. She said you'd bought the old Gallatin place, so . . ."

"Hmm," Daniel grunted sourly. "You and your mother must have had a good laugh about my 'visit to the store.' "

He was uncomfortably close to the truth and Edie felt more than a little ashamed. Hastily changing the subject, she said the first thing that came into her head. "Did your headache last long?"

His voice was muffled as he turned abruptly toward the window. "No longer than usual."

"Do you get them often?"

"Often enough." His clipped reply effectively cut off the subject from further discussion.

A few moments of strained silence passed before he spoke again. "You said yesterday you were 'home for a while.' Home from where?"

"Chicago. We . . . I've lived there for the past nine years."

"Nine—?" He turned to peer at her in the dim light.

Edie answered his unfinished question, smiling faintly. "Thirty-two." His startled reaction was evident. "Oh yes, I'm old enough to vote—and to be a pharmacist," she said pointedly. He swallowed audibly, remembering. "And, evidence to the contrary, I *am* old enough to drive." This time her sarcasm was directed solely at herself.

By now they had turned off the two-lane highway from town onto the access road leading to his house. Beside the darkly glittering lake, waters gleaming in the shadowed nest of tall, thick trees surrounding the shore, it stood, a shade blacker than the sky. Edie pulled up the driveway, tires crunching gravel, the sound loud and alien in the hushed stillness. The motor idled as she waited. Daniel put his hand on the door handle.

He'd never met anyone quite like her before and, though he wanted to, he couldn't deny his curiosity. Actually, it was a rather nice feeling to be interested and curious about *anything*. Still, the warning buzzed in his head, from that first moment she'd been a threat to his control, his solitary retreat from conflict, and he didn't need or want this kind of distraction . . . he needed to be alone, and quiet; there were plans to be made, problems to work out. The most rational, logical step for him was to get away from her as fast as he could. And if one thing could be said of Daniel James Slayton III, it was that he was a rational, logical man. There wasn't an impulsive bone in his body.

And so, astonished, he watched his hand reach out and turn the key in the ignition. The engine's noise died, absorbed into the shadows of the overhanging branches.

Edie stared at him, amazed and apprehensive, the isolated silence thrumming around them. She'd have bet he'd hotfoot it from the car as fast as his long, strong legs could carry him.

"I know it's late," Daniel forestalled her protest, "but since we're neighbors, so to speak, maybe we should try to get off on the right foot." Reluctantly he cast a grim glance at the black bulk of the house on its slight rise next to the ebony shine of the lake. What had always been a welcoming refuge was oppressive and lonely tonight, and warmth and life were here in the compressed confines of a shabby three-year-old Mustang.

He shifted uncomfortably. "Look, I, uh, want to apologize for losing my temper back there." The words were forced, stiff, as if he were setting foot on unknown, untested ground. "A piece of metal can be repaired. It certainly isn't reason enough for rudeness. And this time I can't even use pain as an excuse."

The strain in his voice told Edie what that admission cost this stiff, proud man sitting beside her.

But it wasn't the apology, Daniel knew—though that was certainly out of character. It was the sudden angry outburst of temper itself that had shaken him off balance. It had been a long time since he'd lost his all-but-iron control, with anyone. In truth, he'd never had that much emotion on tap. Or thought he hadn't. He knew how the hospital staff saw him: *The Iceman Cometh*. Frankly, it was the image he fostered, an image he did nothing to discourage.

"Look, perhaps we should . . . uh, get acquainted." At Edie's involuntary snort of disbelief he shook his head. "I know what your opinion of me must be—" When had he ever given a damn about a stranger's opinion? Anyone's opinion. He couldn't figure what the hell had come over him.

Suddenly Edie had to ask. "Uh, excuse me, but you aren't by any chance smiling right now, are you?"

"That's a strange question . . . even from you," he said tartly. "Why?"

"Oh, nothing." Her wistful tone faded. She wished she could have seen it, just once. She turned to look out at the dark silhouette of the house.

"How come your family isn't with you?" As soon as the words were out she wanted to bite off her tongue. She'd probably just ended what might have been an interesting evening. What kind of question was that to ask? It implied an interest she refused to admit, and it was certainly none of her business.

But she waited for his answer. And, when it came, though she couldn't see the bitterness twist his mouth, she heard it clearly enough in his words.

"There is no family. I'm divorced and we didn't have children." Regret and loneliness shadowed his voice, a poignant echo of her own earlier thoughts.

"I'm sorry." For a moment they were caught in the shared intimacy of mutual regret.

Daniel quickly cleared his throat, uncomfortable with even that bit of self-revelation. He veered back to an earlier remark. "You said you live in Chicago. Is your . . . husband with you?"

"I'm not married, either," she answered, eyebrows raised in quiet amusement at his discomfort with the question.

"Oh." A quick release of his pent-up breath was the only visible sign of the sudden lightness he felt. "When you said 'we' lived in Chicago—"

"We did . . . for six years to be precise. He still does, as far as I know." Edie hesitated. "It's been over for quite some time now. Only the divorce is new."

"I'm sorry, I shouldn't have asked. I must be painful for you to talk about."

Good grief! *Two* apologies, and the world was still spinning in orbit. Edie stared hard at Daniel, wishing she could see him more clearly.

"No, not painful really. Well," she smiled to herself ruefully, "maybe a little. But, hey, pain is better than humiliation. Who wants to admit their own stupidity?" She chuckled quietly. "Life's ultimate frustration, when you absolutely, positively cannot find anyone else but yourself to blame. Lately," she muttered wryly, thinking of their first two meetings, "I seem to find myself in that position a lot." She shrugged philosophically. "Ah well, you know what they say—no pain, no gain." *Lord, why was she telling him this? Did he ask?*

Well, yeah, he did. But why should he give a damn? "Now it's my turn to apologize," she said. "I didn't mean to talk your ear off."

"No," he answered quietly, "that's all right. If you want to talk about it, I don't mind." Good God, he meant it! For a moment, shaken, he hoped she wouldn't go on. What business did he have getting entangled in someone else's life?

Edie shrugged again. "I worked in the same hospital where Mark was a resident. Strange, I never could abide a liar, and in that department Mark was really quintessential state-of-the-art." She chuckled. "Ah, but the love of a good woman would change him, said she with her blinders on."

He didn't answer and Edie knew she should shut up, let the poor man get on his way. But the floodgates were open and she couldn't shut off the flow of words. It was a welcome relief to let them loose after all this time. She shook her head, her voice tight with self-mockery.

"Doctors!" He turned abruptly to stare at her obvious disgust. "Funny, isn't it? Thoughtful, intelligent people will completely abdicate their rational thought processes just because 'the doctor says.' Hell, if Hippocrates had known Mark and his friends, he'd have taken up plumbing."

Her tone startled Daniel. "What's wrong with doctors?"

"Oh," she sighed, "certainly not all doctors. It's just Mark and his buddies. For them life was one big seminar in the fine art of cheating . . . on your taxes, the medical insurers, your patients, your wife." Her mouth twisted. "Even your golf score, if you could sink that low."

"But surely you can't tar the entire profession with the same brush because of a bad personal experience!"

"Well . . . of course not." She turned to stare at him, taken aback by his vehemence. "For every Mark Killian there are a hundred decent, honest, dedicated doctors. My mind knows that—it's just going to take a while for the rest of me to catch up: a *long* while!" she laughed.

There was a prolonged silence. "Go on."

"Ah, that's okay. It's late and I'm sure you're tired. You don't have to be polite."

"I am *never* polite. Go on!"

Edie, startled at the harsh order, stared through the darkness at him, but he faced forward, eyes straight ahead. "Yes, I've noticed." She leaned her head back on the seat, a half-smile on her lips. "Well, I can skip the sordid details. He just couldn't believe I actually expected monogamy from him. I mean, he had *soooo* much to give and he only wanted to share the goodies with females less fortunate than I. Oh, the man was generous to a fault." She sounded amazingly cheerful about the whole thing. "Let's just say that a person who lies down like a doormat really shouldn't blame anyone for stepping on them," she said dryly, then straightened and reached toward the ignition key.

"You're a very strong woman," he said after a moment, his words staying her hand.

Daniel wasn't quite sure it was a compliment. He'd known other strong women. His stomach tightened at the memory. They had their commitments and made their decisions, definite and single-minded, and their strength was cold, hard. But not Edie's. And he wondered why. Where lay the difference?

"You have an amazing . . . resilience," he said with grudging admiration. "You can laugh at him, and yourself, even now." He wanted to know her secret, how she'd kept from locking the world away, why she stayed on as a participant in life instead of bitterly stepping back to become an observer on the sidelines.

"I think maybe you've got it backwards," Edie answered, puzzled. "Maybe it was the laughter that made me resilient. It came first, you know. We had a very happy house, my parents and I. I grew up with laughter." He winced, unseen. "I think it just puts that particular lesson in its proper perspective, helps me remember that Mark was only one part of my life, not the sum total." She chuckled. "I believe it's called a learning experience."

How strange, she thought, suddenly startled, even her mother had never been privy to the whole sordid episode with Mark. But Daniel Slayton, he of the cold, critical manner and the appealing, wistful loneliness, he was the one person she'd not hesitated to talk to.

Daniel read some of the emotions tumbling through her thoughts reflected in her face. Even the dim light of the car's interior couldn't camouflage them. She'd never make it at the poker table. And he suddenly realized that was precisely what he was drawn to: Edie's absolute honesty, with him, with herself. From their first meeting there had been not one sign of artifice about Edie Calvin. She exuded an artless simplicity and candor, free of manipulation. She was a tantalizing breath of clean, fresh air after a lifetime in a dungeon of caution and repression.

"You don't play games, do you?"

Edie turned her head, studying him thoughtfully. It was only then he knew he'd spoken.

Though his face was hidden in shadow, she understood exactly what he meant. "No, life's too short and time goes too fast. Truth is truth. Or at least it *should* be!" she muttered fiercely, then stopped, took a deep breath. "What the hell, I figure since I can't avoid it I might just as well face it. Either accept it or change it, but get on with my life. My father always told me to say what you mean and mean what you say. It's much simpler that way—you know who to trust. And people who play games can't be trusted. My legacy from Mark, I suppose." Her hands gripped the wheel with remembered tension, then she sighed. "No, Daniel, I don't play games. Do you?"

It was the first time he'd heard her say his name. The sound of it on her lips was strange, disturbing—a subtle pleasure. He enjoyed listening to the echo of it in his mind. It took a moment for her question to catch up to him. "Do I—? Play games?"

He was startled she'd turned his own probe back on him. He'd never really thought about it. She had a knack for making him think about things he usually avoided. "I suppose so. Everyone knows the rules of the game."

The cynicism of his words pierced the quiet night with an icy thrust. He sounded so cold, she thought, and shivered, a cold that spread outward from his very soul.

Edie ached suddenly for the man beside her whose

loneliness and emptiness echoed in those bleak words. "You know, I find that hard to believe, Daniel. Oh, I'm sure you know the rules all right. Hell, even *I* know them. But, do you believe in them? I thought that's why you're hiding up here, to escape from the game."

My God, she thought suddenly, *that was awful*! What in the world had possessed her to say such a presumptuous thing to him?

"What the hell do you mean—*hiding*? And what business is it of yours what I do?" For a moment the air crackled with the flare of his quick anger.

"You're right, Daniel," Edie said with quiet dignity. "I'm sorry, I had no right to say that. I don't blame you for getting angry. Damn, Mark was right about that, anyway. He always said I had a mouth the size of the Grand Canyon."

Daniel sat quite still for a few uneasy moments, rigid with anger. It faded away as the truth of her words pierced his defenses. He winced, knowing how close she'd come. He ran his fingers raggedly over his closed eyes, wondering if the headache was returning. No, just fatigue, and pressure. Pressure from newly discovered, unanswered, perhaps unanswerable questions.

"God, it's amazing," he muttered wearily. "I never laid eyes on you until twenty-four hours ago and you've managed to raise questions I didn't even know I wanted answered." He sighed. "Strange, isn't it, you don't know me at all, and yet in many ways you seem to understand me better than anyone I've ever known." *Including myself.* "Certainly better than Sandra ever did."

So that was her name, the ex–Mrs. Slayton: Sandra.

They sat quietly, a surprisingly easy silence now. Then Daniel leaned toward Edie and took her hands from the wheel. Holding them firmly in his much larger one, he grasped her shoulder with the other. Turning her so she faced him, he held her motionless.

Edie didn't hear one bell ring; there were no fireworks, no violins. Just a lovely melting warmth, a glowing golden rush of delicious sensation. She sat there, in the familiar confines of her car, and she was lost.

"You know something? I think you're very good for me, Edith Stephanie Calvin. Pardon the expression: just what the doctor ordered."

She stared up into his eyes, mysterious in the darkness. The night had washed the day's color with a subdued palette of black and white and gray, and the silver of his eyes reflected the moon's glitter on dark ripples of water.

Daniel looked at her, the seconds standing still as his breath quickened. His throat was so tight he seemed unable to swallow or get enough air. He moved his hand slowly over her heavy jacket collar, pushing her hair back and baring the side of her neck as he gently rested his fingers against the soft flesh below her jaw. He could feel her pulse throbbing, imitating his own racing heart. Everything about her was so vibrant—so *alive*!

Edie was almost afraid to move. Something crazy was happening to her, and she was afraid to put a name to it. They were suspended somewhere between now and forever, poised on the brink of discovery, waiting for that last breathless moment before the first step of some incredible journey.

Her hands, so gently imprisoned by his, felt a slight tremor and she knew he was as shaken as she. Edie was breathless, weightless, a prickly warmth beginning to ripple over her from a glowing core deep within her body. She felt herself literally coming to life beneath his touch. She leaned slowly toward Daniel, drawn by the tension growing inexorably between them.

He slid his hand over her head, content for the moment to feel the soft springiness of her hair, the fluid texture—*like liquid copper*, he thought—as it twined around his fingers. He pushed his hand through it and her sweet clean scent rose to tease him, the essence of woman, her essence.

Edie felt his quiet breath flutter across her cheek. His mouth brushed hers quickly, softly, and she was caught by the tender delight his kiss surprised there. With unexpected gentleness his lips parted hers. Just for an instant they were still, expectant, and then he began to explore the softness, to learn the velvet texture, the sweet curve, the exciting feel of her under his mouth.

She answered his quest with a sudden rush of hunger, a yearning so intense she felt in danger of losing touch with her world, her life—with everything and everyone except this man she was embracing so fiercely.

Edie's hands made the journey up his arms and over his shoulders, locking around his neck as if they'd found their home. Everything was magnified, all her senses sharpened and expanded. She felt the blood flowing through her veins, the air moving in and out of her lungs, the pores of her skin absorbing the warmth, the scent of Daniel. It was a kiss that swept away every uncertainty she might have had. Stunned, she felt his warm sigh of satisfaction. There was no urgency in their embrace. There was time, all the time they needed. At that moment it seemed there was forever.

"Daniel? Ohhh, Daniel," Edie sighed, her lips feathering his temple. And then she just forgot to form any more words with her mouth. She was far too busy doing other things, suddenly enthralled with the texture of his skin, the way the sandpaper roughness at his jaw softened ever so slightly over the curve of his upper lip. She touched her tongue to the slight indentation just above it and felt his shuddering response. Her lips caressed the taut flesh that crested the ridge of his cheek-bone and became the soft, intricate curve of his earlobe.

Compelled by a dimension of desire too strong to deny, Edie's hands moved restlessly across the thick wool of Daniel's jacket. At the edge of her mind danced the enchanting memory of their first meeting, and that moment when her hands explored this same body, and how it felt without the intervening layer of bulky cloth. Damn these cold Michigan nights!

Edie's shaking hands slid along Daniel's head to nest in the spill of thick dark hair, impatient fingers fluttered over his hot skin. A day's growth of bristle along the hard line of his jaw scraped the sensitive flesh of her palms and even that caused its own special shiver of sensation.

It was the crackling of the paper bag, crushed between them, that broke through the misty haze and suddenly thrust unwelcome reality into the overheated interior of the small car.

"What the hell—!"

FOUR

"What the hell—!"

Edie followed Daniel's eyes as he stared down at the crumpled bag resting against his knee.

Its contents seeped through the paper, and they watched the ice cream inch its way down the length of his pant leg. A narrow white trickle reached his ankle, beginning to collect in his hand-sewn imported black leather shoe.

"Ice cream," Edie muttered.

"Yes." Daniel nodded his head as if that explained everything. He sat very still, staring at his foot.

"It was Lorraine's dessert," she mumbled.

"I could collect the rest of it—there's another shoe that hasn't even been touched," Daniel answered tartly. "She could drink it like champagne."

Edie flinched. There was no need for sarcasm. Well, from his point of view, perhaps there was.

Daniel looked out at the black sky, stars invisible behind the clouds. The moon's light and the glare of the headlights illuminated only a small part of the darkness surrounding them. His left leg, damp and sticky, felt distinctly uncomfortable. It was a feeling his whole psyche was suddenly sharing with the unfortunate leg. And then the corner of his mouth moved, a slight twitch. He bit his lips. At last, unable to contain it, he threw back his head, and a huge burst of laughter filled the car.

Edie gaped. She had wanted so very much to see him smile, but laughter—especially now!—was beyond all expectations. It was as if a dam had burst, flooding through his dark thoughts, washing them clean, and bringing sunshine in their place. His laughter tugged at Edie's heart because she sensed how very rare a thing it was.

Daniel looked at her, then down at the soggy mess, and when he returned his eyes to her face, the last knot of tension dissolved. Her own nervous chuckle gave way to shared laughter.

"Well," he said carefully, "it's not as effective as a cold shower, but it'll do." He opened the car door. "And this time I advise you to drive home more carefully," Daniel admonished sternly as he climbed from the car, stepping gingerly on his soggy shoe.

Even then she might have reached out to hold him, she admitted to herself in annoyance. But the sticky wet puddle spreading to her own leg wrenched her back to reality. A cold, wet reality, Edie saw in disgust, a reality that would leave a large stain on her upholstery.

Good grief! She looked at him, beside the still-open door. What had she done? She thought of the difficult months since the divorce, her slow but steady progress back to herself. Dear God, what had she *undone*?

"Thanks for the warning but you really don't have to tell me how to drive. You don't have to tell me anything. Just . . . please, just leave me alone." Her words were abrupt and suddenly cool in the still-heated atmosphere of the car. He slammed the door firmly behind him, staring at her thoughtfully through the window. He didn't bother to answer, just turned away up the shadowed walk to the dark, waiting house. Reluctantly, Edie thought he managed to look very dignified, and sexy, despite one soaked pant leg clinging stickily and the other, ripped beyond repair, flapping in the breeze.

She stared after him, bemused, her own words echoing in her ears, and watched him disappear inside the door. Arms folded over the steering wheel, Edie rested her weary head for a moment. *Leave me alone*, she'd demanded: she almost had to smile. More likely the other way around. He should be telling her to leave *him* alone. *She* had done most of the damage. But what kind of damage was worse? She recalled her steamy, unpredictable response to him, appalled at her feverish arousal under his hands, his mouth—

Oh, Calvin, you are so stupid! You've just managed to escape an almost completely destructive marriage. Yes, her beleaguered rational self agreed, *she had*. Right, and here she was getting involved again. Would she always be a pushover for every sexy-looking pair of pants that came down the pike?

No. *No.* And yet some instinct warned her there was more, very much more than that to Daniel Slayton. But did she dare to find out what? Her fists clenched and she clamped her jaw. She felt as if she'd just been seduced by the devil. Sure, she thought wildly, the devil made me do it!

Swiftly, Edie shoveled the sticky mess down onto the washable floor mat and gunned the motor. With a squeal of tires she fled blindly, as if from that very devil, backing down Daniel's driveway and flinching as she recalled the way she'd backed into his Jaguar—was it only a couple of hours ago? An eternity. And look where it had got her. *Sorry, Mom, didn't watch where I was going*. Again.

A worried, agitated Edie retraced the miles back into town. Every click of the odometer made her more determined to wrest back her self-control from the hands of that . . . that Svengali! Well, too damn bad. He's not going to find his Trilby living in *this* part of Michigan. No sirree.

Edie glanced down at the soggy remains of Lorraine's late-lamented dessert and jeered at herself. Saved from the proverbial fate worse than . . . and she had the laziest, spoiled-rottenest dog on God's green earth to thank!

The door closed quietly behind Daniel, shutting him inside his dark, silent cocoon of isolation. Automatically he slipped off his shoes, thinking suddenly how much he hated this house. Funny. Until tonight his prized solitude had been exactly what he'd loved most about it. But now . . .

The loud burst of noise from Edie's car, the desperate screech of tires as she escaped down the drive disturbed his reverie. He knew exactly how she felt, he thought wryly. But he had the strangest feeling there was no place to run, nowhere to hide. And did he want to? Hadn't he done enough running, enough hiding?

That he could even ask the question was answer enough.

Daniel wandered along the dark hall into the large room stretching along one entire side of the house. An expanse of windows faced the lovely panorama of lake, trees, and sky, flooded now with the ghostly white shine of the three-quarter moon. A few wisps of cloud scudded across its partial face as he stared up, seeing another face, one that seemed to have taken a permanent lease on his thoughts.

He recalled Edie's expression as she was held by the pain of her own unpleasant memories, and then when she listened and considered his words, there in the car. Listened, and heard. Among the people with whom he'd spent his life, none of them ever cared enough to *listen*. But then, he ruefully asked himself, when had he?

But Edie Calvin had seemed to care, really care about him, his pain. *Well, hell, she'd care about any suffering animal*, he taunted himself. *Don't take it so personally*.

But there, of course, was the problem. He *was* taking Edie personally—very personally.

She'd worked a minor miracle tonight, he mused. They had shared laughter. Laughter! Damn, it was almost beyond memory, the last time he'd felt that kind of unrestrained joyousness. He wondered, had he *ever* felt it quite like that? For that short time he'd completely forgotten the painful and urgent problems, the cold, stark parameters his life had shrunk to.

Those minutes with Edie were a refreshing oasis in the arid landscape of his life. And, perversely, in that one fleeting instant, Daniel almost hated her—hated her for forcing him to see what he was missing, what he'd always missed. All those years, stretching back, and back, suddenly empty and bleak, the accomplishments now so meaningless. How had he managed even this long in that superficial, artificial, goddam empty world? In the space of those few minutes with Edie Calvin he'd shared more honest emotion, more tenderness, more real passion that he'd known in an entire lifetime. It was a frightening and uncomfortable reminder.

Daniel picked up his discarded shoes and with heavy steps walked back to the stairs. Turning on the light in the spacious and utterly immaculate bedroom, he looked around with a stranger's eyes. ''A place for everything and everything in its place.'' There'd been a warning, an inherent fear not well hidden beneath that stern childhood lesson. No clutter, no disruption of her life and her comforts would be permitted by the mistress of that household. Not by her husband, her servants, her child. It had been drummed into Daniel's brain by housekeepers, maids, butlers, his mother's obedient, conscientious, and well-paid surrogates.

Now, taking stock of the neat, uncluttered, uncomfortably sterile room, Daniel was suddenly aware of how little he'd traveled from boyhood and those early years.

His mouth thinned as he reflected on the house he'd grown up in. He hadn't *lived* there: one merely occupied space in a house like that. The inhabitants . . . he couldn't consider the word "family" in that context . . . even the very young Daniel, had known unseemly behavior was frowned upon by the joyless woman who reigned in that house. And under the heading "unseemly" was an extremely long list. There had been precious little opportunity for laughter.

Suddenly recalling the sticky ooze congealing inside his shoe, Daniel shook his head as he viewed the mottled leather. He dropped the shoes into the wastebasket, where they were soon joined by the remains of his ruined pants. He began to remove the rest of his clothing as he continued his curiously detached survey.

No matter how much he detested that house, that life, he'd never really shaken himself loose. Like a turtle, he carried it around with him, to crawl back to when the rest of the world came too close.

His eyes were drawn once more to the wastebasket and he stood, hand frozen in the act of removing his sweater. He stared thoughtfully, the frown disappearing as his brooding expression softened.

His mouth turned upward. Maybe he'd come a bit farther than he'd thought. And for the second time that evening he heard the rusty sound of his own laughter. He bent slowly to retrieve the ruined remains, setting them gently on the pristine surface of the dresser. Daniel couldn't stop smiling—maybe he'd have them bronzed!

He sank down on the bed and lay spread-eagled across its width, staring blindly at the ceiling. All he could see was the laughing, lovely face of the woman who had burst into the dark prison of his life with all the sunshine brightness of a summer day. He experienced a vivid picture of Edie in this room with him. His body tightened, remembering how it had felt, his mouth touching, tasting, his hands moving across her soft, sweet skin. He threw his arm across his eyes, trying to shut out the tantalizing vision, smile faltering, fingers closing into a hard fist.

No! There were too many obstacles in front of him, he would *not* go looking for another one to fall over. Not after the royal screwup he'd already made of his life. No, the best thing for him was to avoid Edie Calvin like the plague. Despite the smallness of the town, it shouldn't be too difficult; he was quite good at avoiding things.

The room, and the night, seemed suddenly colder than ever.

Edie paced her room, as restless as a caged animal. She wasn't comfortable with her thoughts, the wild sensations she unwillingly relived.

No, she just wasn't ready for this. Ha! She might never be *ready* for Daniel Slayton. Well, she was just going to have to work on her resistance . . . which obviously needed a lot of work.

She came to rest in front of her dresser, eyeing herself with disfavor in the old wood-framed mirror. "There will not—I repeat, *not*—be a rerun of this evening." The flushed face of the reflection appeared decidedly unconvinced. "Yeah, but, on the other hand," Edie mused doubtfully, "maybe there's nothing wrong with a little old-fashioned lust, hmmm?" The skeptical face looked back.

"Look," she earnestly tried to convince herself, "isn't it the perfect solution? You can bet *he* doesn't want anything more than that. And I sure don't. But I might be able to handle a little heavy breathing."

She sighed. It might sound like the answer but, frankly, Edie doubted her follow-through. Ah, now there was the rub. In every sport she'd ever played, elementary school to college and beyond, it was the coaches' eleventh commandment: "Thou shalt follow through."

But this was not a game, she reminded herself sharply. And, for a moment, she was back in the car with Daniel, hearing her own solemn words. *No*, she sighed to the worried woman behind the glass, *irresistible impulses and all, this is definitely real life.*

"I'm trapped, just like you in your glass cage."

Suddenly she gripped the edge of the dresser and shook her head vehemently, glaring at her image. "Well, *you* may be trapped but I sure as hell am not!" Edie swung around, addressing the lamp on the bedside table. "I don't need this! I'm just beginning to get my life in order. I'm starting to *like* myself again, and I'm not going to louse up my freedom with any more undesirable elements."

Four steps brought her to the window, and a wry smile crossed her lips. She shrugged sheepishly at the small rocking chair that stood there. "Okay, okay . . . I admit it, the *last* word for Daniel Slayton is undesirable." She retraced her restless steps around the small room in a failed effort to find some token refuge and came to a dead stop opposite the door to the hall. She stared accusingly at the long-patient face of Lorraine lying on the threshold as if she'd taken root.

The dog's fixed gaze pinned Edie in mid-stride, as though she wondered what her crazy human was all excited about now! Edie dropped to her knees, cradling the dog in her lap and resting her cheek on top of Lorraine's bony head. "You must think people are really nuts, huh, sweetie? Always running around in circles, making noise, getting all hot and bothered, when any intelligent canine knows that chasing your own tail is useless, wasted energy."

The two-legged female nodded sagely at her four-legged counterpart. "And you know what, you're right." Edie rested her head against the wall and her muttered words were directed at the doorknob, which, until now, had managed to stay out of the discussion. "I mean, what the heck, maybe all this frenzied agonizing is for nothing . . . the electricity may fizzle."

And if it doesn't? Edie glared at the dog, who was now yawning, apparently bored to tears with all this foolishness.

"This is all your fault, you know that, don't you? You lazy, useless, spoiled excuse for a woman's best friend. You and your ice cream. *You* made me what I am today: an indecisive, crying, clumsy, weak-kneed, miserable . . . AAARGH! I could just *scream*!"

FIVE

In the last two weeks, Daniel mused, the late fall weather had taken an erratic turn for the worse. So had his temper. He chose to avoid analysis at the moment and, instead, shoved open the car door, emerging into a wind tinged with the imminent arrival of an icy northern blast. Hunched down into his jacket, collar turned up over his ears, leather-gloved hands stuffed in his pockets, he trudged across the sidewalk. The heavy glass door, rimmed with bright red and green neon, glowed with a beckoning hospitality, transient though it might be. He opened the door and was was enveloped in the noise, bright lights, and tantalizing aroma of Gus's Pizza Palace.

A gray-haired woman hurried across the pavement, head lowered against the wind. Her foot hit an errant patch of ice and she slid into him, propelling him precipitately through the door.

"Whoa there, slow down," Daniel steadied her. "You that hungry?" He was relieved to see she wasn't hurt.

"Oh, I'm so sorry. I didn't mean to sweep you off

your feet.'' Her cheerful laugh was laced with embarrassment.

"It's all right, I'm getting used to it.'' His wry expression caught her attention—and she beamed at her victim.

"Why, you're Mr. Slayton, aren't you?''

Daniel was used to the lack of anonymity in Pecomish Springs, although, he reflected with satisfaction he had no complaints on that score. He'd managed, with a singularly determined effort, to sink out of sight and out of mind every summer for the past six years since he'd bought the house. He nodded his head at the woman. "Yes, Daniel Slayton. And you . . . ?''

"Oh, that's right, we've never met. I'm Lillian Calvin.''

Well, she had his attention *now*. Daniel's surprise became one of fatalistic recognition. It was accompanied by the sick, strangled smile of a man who, without further struggle, gamely accepts whatever destiny a capricious fate has decreed.

"Of course you are.'' He sighed. The bright amber-flecked eyes, the alert tilt of her head, the once russet hair now liberally streaked with gray. "You have a daughter.'' There was a wealth of unspoken meaning in those four words.

"Yes! I believe you've met Edie, haven't you?''

"In a manner of speaking,'' Daniel mumbled.

"She mentioned you'd been in the store.'' They moved to the take-out counter, making small talk while waiting for their orders, and Lillian took the opportunity to look more closely at Daniel. Edie's late arrival home two weeks ago, her mumbled explanation of the car accident, the muffled argument she'd carried on with herself and her bedroom furniture had not gone unnoticed. Lillian gazed at the apparent cause of the turmoil; instinctively she liked him. She had *never* liked Mark Killian.

Lillian noted the small box holding Daniel's pizza and, with a mother's unerring instinct, took a decisive step right into the middle of her daughter's muddled affairs.

"Are you eating alone?" she asked abruptly.

"Uh, well, yes I am."

"Good!"

Daniel raised his brows, wondering why his solitude should be a source of satisfaction to her.

"Why don't you join us? Two's company but three's fun. And with company you'll digest better."

Better than what? The daughter's crazy and the mother's a cannibal.

Oh come on! He was beginning to feel like Alice on the other side of the looking glass.

But the thought of another solitary meal was at that moment distinctly unappetizing. "Why, thank you. That sounds great."

Seeing Edie Calvin again sounded even better. He'd fought his instincts and it hadn't done much good. Who was he fooling?

The evening was definitely looking up.

Edie applied the large terry-cloth towel to the damp remains of her shower and wrapped another around her freshly shampooed hair. She scowled at the shampoo bottle on the counter: she'd have to change brands. That one had too many disturbing associations. She couldn't forget how it and the cotton balls had clung stickily to Daniel's jacket on their first meeting. Ah well.

Zipping up the velour bathrobe, she ran down the stairs and hurried into the kitchen. With the practiced skill of a Las Vegas blackjack dealer, she dealt out a pair of paper plates and napkins across the surface of the table.

Finished, her glance flickered over the telephone on the wall. Hmph! She was *glad* he hadn't called. Who needed him, anyway? She was free. She didn't want any entanglements.

And she couldn't lie worth a damn.

When she heard the key in the lock, Edie had everything ready, everything except her defenses. Which was why, when the door opened, her mouth dropped open so inelegantly. She stared into the cool gleam of the gray eyes facing her above the head of a suspiciously smug-looking Lillian.

My God, I let myself think about him for one instant and now he's standing at the door! Then she saw the extra box from the pizzeria.

"Guess who's coming to dinner?" Edie muttered.

"Darling, isn't this nice?" Lillian exclaimed. "We bumped into each other at Gus's."

Lillian and Daniel exchanged the understanding smiles of two who shared a private joke and Edie waited, puzzled, as they closed the door.

"Your mother is," he said wryly, "unmistakably, your mother. She slid on some ice, right into me."

Edie groaned.

"That's when she recognized me." His expression didn't change. "You know, from your description of *our* first meeting?"

He didn't sound very disturbed, she realized. Why, he was actually *enjoying* this. She'd walked around like a zombie for two weeks, on edge and itchy, as if sand ran in her veins instead of blood, waiting for the damned phone to ring. And *he* was perfectly relaxed and feeling just fine, thank you very much!

"We Calvin women bowl men over at the very first meeting. It's taken years to learn how, but practice makes perfect," she grumbled, grabbing the boxes from his hands. "Don't worry, the effect wears off fast!" *Obviously*. Edie slammed the pizzas down on the table with a fervor she wished, irrationally, she could exercise on his head instead of the innocent slab of wood.

Daniel slid out of his jacket, watching her with hungry intensity, his heart lurching dangerously. He noted her flushed cheeks and the stray tendrils of damp hair that had escaped the confines of her terry turban. His imagination did terrible things to his blood pressure as her body moved beneath the softly clinging robe. He was uncomfortably aware that there was probably nothing between her and her velour. Even the presence of her *mother*, for God's sake, did nothing to discourage his reaction!

"Uh, Edie dear, why don't you go comb your hair while we wash up?" Lillian suggested brightly, hanging up her and Daniel's coats beside the back door.

Ohmigosh! Edie suddenly had a very clear picture of her appearance. "Ah . . . yes! That's a—a very good idea, Mom." Calmly she moved to the door. The minute she crossed the threshold her bare feet grew wings and she flew up to her room, tossing the towel onto the bed as she looked for her brush. Then she blushed, realizing just how provocative a sight she presented and, gritting her teeth, reached first for her bra.

Underwear, she decided, was marvelous protection. But against what, she wondered, Daniel or herself? Because there was definitely room for doubt, she was honest enough to admit that. Shaking her head in annoyance, Edie returned to the mirror. Oh that hair! Why, just once, couldn't she run into Daniel (bad choice of words there) when she was poised, well-groomed, desirable (a worse choice). Good grief, why should she worry about "desirable"?

Oh Edie, you fool, don't even ask!

Edie recognized, without understanding, this strange contradiction in her response to Daniel Slayton. *She wanted him; she didn't want him.* All the daisies in the world wouldn't give her that answer. She'd have to reach the solution in her own way.

They say getting there is half the fun.

A few minutes with the blow dryer did wonders for her appearance and her self-confidence. As she reached for a shirt and jeans, she suddenly stopped, and grinned. The mischievous devil inside demanded the indulgence of sudden impulse.

Cooly she slipped her robe back on, smoothing the soft, lustrous fabric over her body with a delicious shiver of anticipation. A few moments later a much more decorous Edie glided into the kitchen on satin bedroom slippers, in control and ready to fight, with herself if necessary, to keep it that way.

Daniel looked up from the sink when he heard her steps and his eyes widened with delight. The russet glow of her softly curled hair shone in the light, a nimbus around her head, gleaming with a life of its own. Edie's cheeks were still faintly flushed from her recent headlong flight upstairs, and her eyes were bright with a kind of suppressed excitement. He couldn't take his eyes from her mouth, slightly parted and smiling under its glistening shine of lipstick.

Daniel suddenly saw her as the truly lovely woman she was, and he realized with a start this was the first time he'd seen Edie like this. In the store she'd been . . . cute, messy, spirited, and undeniably dirty! And in the car, the darkness had lent her distance, even mystery, an almost ghostly sensuality.

But in the brightly lit, homey atmosphere of this old-fashioned, slightly shabby kitchen, stood a golden, glowing woman, filled with vibrant life, real and warm. He felt a surging need to touch that sweet scrubbed skin, to push his fingers through the bright copper mass of curls, to feel that smiling mouth once more twist with passion under his own.

Edie's pulse stopped for an instant, then skidded into a double-time race through her veins, the noise so loud in her ears she'd have sworn anyone within a block could hear. She felt his steady gaze, felt it in the heat coursing through her blood, felt it in the tightening breasts, the sharp coil of sensation in her body. Only the increasingly painful pressure of her nails digging into her palms kept her mind on a rational level and her traitorous body from melting onto the kitchen linoleum. She was perversely angry with herself, and *him*, for her wanton thoughts and her spineless reaction.

She never knew what she might have said or done if Lillian, still innocent of the crackling tension in the room, hadn't turned just then and noticed her daughter frozen in the doorway.

"Oh Edie, there you are. What happened to the beer? I'd have sworn there was one left to give Daniel."

"I used it to rinse my hair," Edie answered waspishly, glad to be able to deny him *something*, even something as minor as a beer. Beer! No doubt *he'd* prefer Dom Perignon. Probably ate pizza with a knife and fork. Stuffy. Money and manners, and *stuffy*. She knew his kind.

Oh, that's really childish, she scolded herself. *Grow up!* But the electricity that had flared sent shafts of real fear right through her heart and she was very much afraid she could find this situation, this man, too hot to handle.

Two weeks. He could have called!

"Oh well, that's all right. I was afraid you'd given it to Lorraine. You know how she gets after a beer. No telling how it'll affect her." Lillian looked at Daniel, motioning him to the table. "It's okay at bedtime but now is still too early. She'd probably fall asleep right into her dish." She laughed indulgently and went on setting out ice cubes and soft drinks. "Where is she, by the way?" She glanced at Edie, who was adding another plate and napkin to the table.

"Who knows?" she shrugged. "Gone into hiding until the food is served. You know Sweet Lorraine, one whiff and she'll drag her fat, lazy a . . . er, bones in here as fast as those chubby little legs can carry her."

Daniel was grateful for the diversion, relieved to focus on a less stimulating object than Edie. Now, as he listened, he could hardly *wait* to meet this paragon of femininity. Lorraine sounded like a real prize.

"Is she older or younger than you?" he asked Edie while Lillian hunted in a drawer crammed to the rim with an assortment of strange implements.

Edie stared, perplexed at the strange question. Then, understanding dawned, the impish twinkle in her eyes belying the artless answer. "In actual years she's younger, but she's been on the loose so long she's got much more . . . experience than I do. It's always been difficult to keep her close to home." She sighed bravely. "Poor Mom and Dad, they couldn't do a thing with Lorraine. I mean, she's always been so hard to control."

Warming to the game, Edie went on. "Of course, it's begun to tell on her lately. She's let herself go and everything just kind of . . . *sags*. The body can stand only so much abuse, after all." After a deliberate but very expressive shudder Edie smiled brightly at Daniel, who by now had an unpleasantly clear picture of the still-absent Lorraine.

"Oh, she'll be *so* glad you're here." Edie clasped her hands in front of her, an angelic smile on her lips. "You know, living in a house with only women, she really misses a man's touch. I only hope she restrains her enthusiasm a bit. If she really takes a liking to you, she wouldn't even be bashful about sitting on your lap or . . . well, I'm afraid when she gets carried away she tends to—" She paused, a poignant catch in her voice, and shook her head. "Not a pretty sight."

"Ah, here it is . . . I knew I'd find it!" caroled a victorious Lillian, holding up the pizza cutter.

By now Daniel wore a sick smile on his face. He

thought Edie's expression looked quite peculiar. Her mouth was twitching and she seemed to have difficulty speaking. Well, no wonder! The strain of coping with a sister like that must be tremendous. This Lorraine was a real cross for them to bear. And yet they seemed to have a genuine love for her. They went out of their way to pamper her . . . ice cream, beer. Perhaps a little less pampering would have been better! He hoped Lorraine's all-powerful nose would stay out of commission a while longer, until he could make a graceful departure. Meeting her was a pleasure he would gladly forgo.

Lillian looked over his shoulder and smiled affectionately. "Ah, here she is. Where have you been, sweetie?"

Daniel steeled himself for the introduction. He had a disconcerting vision of smothering beneath a large, drunken, wrinkled behemoth, his neck nuzzled with sodden affection. He glanced at Edie as she daintily bit into her pizza and wondered how two sisters could be so different.

Now he turned his head, masking his distaste, and was mystified to see an empty doorway. Suddenly a heavy weight settled atop his feet and, startled, he looked down. His mouth fell open in incredulity. It was a few seconds before his reactions caught up with his racing thoughts.

"A . . . dog. *Lorraine is a DOG*?" His gray eyes were wide in dumb amazement at his own error, and his mouth gaped as his feet disappeared beneath the brown and white heap of wrinkles that settled its bulk slowly under his chair.

Edie tried vainly to control her laughter, the intermittent giggles and stifled gasps gurgling from her throat. She finally gave in to it, enjoying Daniel's discomfort with a relish she ought to have been ashamed of.

A dull red stain slashed his high cheekbones as Lillian looked up from her plate with an innocent smile. "Of course she's a dog. What did you think she was, my sister?"

"No," Edie gasped, on a fresh spasm of laughter, "he thought she was *my* sister."

Lillian frowned suspiciously. "That's silly, you don't have a sister."

Daniel, with enviable restraint, closed his eyes and shook his head. With deliberate precision he forced open the fist he'd unconsciously clenched in the first spurt of anger, loosening the fingers one by one, as he carefully released one of his feet from its furry prison.

"Just what," he inquired, "did you do for laughs before I stumbled into your life?" For the moment he was managing to control the impulse to throttle Edie Calvin. It would upset her mother, no doubt, and he had nothing against *her*. Yet. If what he'd seen so far was normal behavior for her daughter, the poor woman had enough to contend with.

Considering the staid and sober conduct of his life, and the fact that it was unthinkable that decorous Daniel James Slayton III should *ever* be the butt of anyone's joke, his tone was masterfully restrained. Here he was, still in his seat, faintly puzzled to find himself there, and looking with fascination at the grinning, teary-eyed, red-faced woman who had so quickly become the bane of his existence.

"Oh, I *am* sorry, Daniel," Edie gulped, wiping her eyes and taking a deep breath. Had she gone too far? "That was mean. Please forgive me, but I just couldn't resist, it was such a perfect setup." She smiled appealingly and reached out to touch his hand resting between them on the table.

Without thought he grasped hers firmly, succumbing for an instant to the feel of her warm, smooth skin under his fingers. Anger was no barrier in the face of the sensations surging through him, overcoming his resistance and reserve. And in the depths of her glowing eyes he saw she felt it, too, this unfathomable pull between them.

"Are you going to force me to eat all this myself? Because, I warn you, I'll do it." Lillian's amused tolerance in view of their mutual distraction was obvious, and they smiled sheepishly.

"You owe me one." Daniel mouthed the words silently at Edie across the table, and they started making hasty inroads on the food in front of them.

Daniel swallowed a bite of pizza—eating it with his fingers, Edie noticed with chagrin. "How did you happen to name her Lorraine? She doesn't look like a Lorraine."

Lillian's smile took on a tender, faintly sad look of reminiscence as she reached down to stroke the dog's head.

"Edie's father, Jacob, and I grew up here. I'd known him all my life, although he was a few years older. He was in the army during World War II, and I decided that when he finally came back I'd be grown up and ready for him. And I was!" She laughed with delight at the memory. "He never stood a chance, although it took a while to convince him. Finally one night he took me to a dance and that's when he asked me to marry him." Her thoughts turned inward for a moment, to that young girl and her soldier in the first flush of their love.

"Where was I? Oh, yes, Lorraine. Well, we were dancing to that song, 'Sweet Lorraine,' when I finally caught him." Her voice softened. "That was always our song: Nat 'King' Cole singing 'Sweet Lorraine.'" Lillian smiled fondly at her listeners, then down at the dog. "So, we've always had a Lorraine. That's what we named every dog we ever had." She sniffled a bit, cleared her throat, and popped a slice of pepperoni into her mouth.

"That's," Daniel's voice caught, "quite a story. Thank you for telling me." He stopped for a moment, strangely moved by her words, then quickly shook off the queer feeling, embarrassed and unsure in the grip of unfamiliar emotions. "Does she eat pizza?" He looked down into the sad canine face staring up from beside his left ankle.

"Oh no, Daniel, don't give her that, it's your dinner. She'll eat anything that isn't nailed down."

"Now, Edith, don't exaggerate." Lillian shook her head. "She's just got a . . . healthy appetite. And anyway, she does, too, have discriminating taste. She won't touch liver and onions." She winked at Daniel, then took another healthy bite of her pizza.

"Well, there you are." Edie shrugged expressively. "Some gourmet. Why, liver and onions," she kissed her fingers, "that's food for the gods! I remember a restaurant in Chicago—"

"Ely's! Right?" Daniel grinned triumphantly at her surprise and they nodded at each other in emphatic and delighted agreement.

"You've been there! Isn't it great?"

"Yes, quite a few times. I remember once when I was at Michael Reese Hospital, I'd just finished my first year of residency and—"

The sudden silence filled the room like a living presence, broken only by the sound of Lorraine demolishing her dinner, and Edie's indrawn breath. Lillian stared in dismay at Daniel, well aware of her daughter's antipathy toward the medical profession.

"Ahem," Lillian coughed delicately. "You'd better eat up before it gets cold, Daniel." Automatically he picked up the wedge of pizza, holding it but making no attempt to eat. He just stared at Edie, who seemed to be having a great deal of trouble swallowing. She stared back. The silence congealed, as thick as the mozzarella.

Abruptly Lillian launched herself from the table. She had no desire to remain in what threatened at any moment to become a combat zone.

"You two just stay where you are. I'm . . . uh, I'm going to . . . take Lorraine for a walk!" She made a cowardly escape, dragging her reluctant furry friend after her, before either of the other two could protest. But they were only marginally aware of her departure, so intent were they on each other.

"You're a doctor?" Edie asked quietly.

"Well, yes, a cardiac surgeon, actually."

Her look of distaste was obvious. "I see."

"Edie, you don't have to look at me as if I'd just crawled out from under a rock."

"Your words, not mine," she said. "Why didn't you say anything? You knew how I felt, I told you."

Daniel tore his unhappy gaze from her face. "Because this is exactly what I thought would happen. I wanted," he looked at her again, pinned by her accusing stare, "I wanted us to be friends. Then I would have told you."

Edie folded her hands in her lap. "I don't want to be 'friends' with you. I don't want to be *anything* with you. You lied—" At his protest she amended, "Oh, maybe you didn't lie but you didn't tell the truth, either, and it's the same thing in my book. You can't help the medical degree but you could have been honest." She stopped, sighed. "No, I guess you couldn't. I've found those two things have no relationship." She stood up. "And neither do we."

"Don't you think you're being unreasonable?"

Unreasonable. "Just go home. Please." Her mouth and her eyes were hard as she reached for the box lying open on the table. She shoved it to the edge and tipped its contents into his unsuspecting lap. "And take your pizza with you." Edie walked from the kitchen, her cool words trailing behind her.

Stunned, Daniel stared at the remains of his dinner spread across his lap, his shirt bearing matching red splotches of sauce. His face hardened, his own anger beginning to erupt once the initial shock wore off. He'd certainly had ample provocation, ever since his first glimpse of her, and his control was wearing dangerously thin. A scowl darkened his face.

With shaking hands he cleaned the food off his clothes, dumped the mess into the garbage, and, old habits dying hard, cleaned the table of its refuse. When the kitchen was in a state of inordinate neatness Lillian wouldn't have recognized, Daniel stalked to the door, ready to wash his hands of this crazy family . . . human, canine, and God knew what else!

But the heat of rage had cooled and in its wake was a sense of frustration and loss, and just plain stubbornness. Because she was foolish and impulsive and close-minded, that didn't mean she should get away with it. Dammit, she was *wrong*.

Daniel turned abruptly and went back to the front hall. "Edie," he called. Then once more, "Edie!" Silence was the only answer. Resolute, he headed up the stairs: he'd just have to *make* her listen to him. One door was closed and he assumed it belonged to Edie. Closed, just like her mind. Under any other circumstances he would certainly have waited for her to answer his knock. But he was in the grip of stronger emotions than he'd ever experienced. Right now it was sincere, righteous anger.

He pounded on the door and, in the same instant, turned the knob, flinging open the door with almost no warning.

SIX

At the closet door, Edie swung around to face an irate Daniel. "Wh-what are you doing here? What do you want?" The words, meant as an accusation, emerged in a hesitant whisper.

Emotion, thought, wild instinct all churned together, focused on Daniel, standing here, so close. Too close. Edie stood poised in mid-gesture, hands flung outward, ineffectual barriers. The slight protection of the night-gown she'd put on was a flimsy shield, covering, with an intimate caress, the lush curves of her body. It was as explicit as a second skin.

In Daniel's gaze it was a trifling obstacle, only enhancing sudden desire. If hatred was akin to love, then it seemed anger was very close to passion. The right-eous temper that impelled him up the stairs was trans-formed now into another, more acute sensation. The sight of her, the very real, very physical embodiment of his midnight visions, cracked his control.

For a frozen instant they stood, separated by five feet of pale blue carpet, and as close as a heartbeat. Edie's body was warmed with his presence, chilled with antici-pation. How, she wondered dazedly, could she be hot and cold at the same time? She didn't know, and it didn't matter. She heard her own quick, shallow breathing, the racing thud of her pulse.

Transfixed, she stared at Daniel, his hand still holding the gleaming brass doorknob. His gray eyes, glittering now with a feverish intensity, were fixed on her; they held her, told her things she was longing to discover and yet afraid to hear. He filled the room, though he didn't move an inch, and she saw his breathing was as labored as hers.

"Edie . . ."

His hoarse groan echoed in the silence, shattering the queer spell, bringing her back to the reality that had disappeared with his entrance. She edged sideways to the bed and hastily grabbed her robe from where she'd tossed it, and held it protectively in front of her, lifting her chin defiantly.

"What do you want, Daniel? This *is* my bedroom—I should think you'd have the good manners to respect my privacy!"

After that first stunned moment Daniel's enviable mastery of emotion stood him in good stead. "I'm not sure," he said quietly, "that you're the best person to teach good manners."

Daniel's voice was low but inflexible. He moved forward and Edie stepped back, alarmed at the implacable resolve in his face. The edge of the bed warned her further retreat was impossible.

Daniel frowned. "I thought you prided yourself on your professionalism. You're a pharmacist—have you forgotten everything you learned about the scientific method? You know, test the theory for *proof* before you make a final decision. Did you conveniently forget that along the way?" His set jaw, the rigidity of his body, both showed the effort he was exerting to keep his feelings in check, an effort he'd never *needed* before because the feelings hadn't ever been aroused.

But Edie was still caught in the throes of her own confusion, compounded by the hurt and disappointment she felt. Daniel had deceived her. That was all she could focus on.

"I've learned a lot of things, and I haven't forgotten any of them. I still know a liar when I see one, Doctor Slayton." Edie closed her eyes for a moment and the adrenaline surged again. "What are you doing up here in the boondocks, anyway?" she taunted. "Don't you have a practice——a nice *lucrative* practice, of course, that's obvious." Her tone was cynical and her eyes raked his expensive clothing, remembering his car, the air about him that fairly shouted "money."

The emotional outburst, denied far too long, burst forth, many months and miles from the man who'd earned it. She knew, in some hidden corner of her brain, *knew* it was aimed at the wrong man and was perversely unable to stem the flood of accusations.

"What charm can a one-horse hick town like this hold for you? Haven't you amused yourself long enough with us locals?" The words rushed on, strung together on a thin thread of sarcasm. "Why don't you go back where you belong, with your Jaguars and gold watches and tax shelters, and women falling all over you . . . all the nice perks that come with that 'Doctor.' "

"Stop trying so hard to be a shrew, Edie." His impatience was reflected in the darkening gray storm of his eyes, the almost painful grip he had on her arms. "You seem to have an abysmally low opinion of the medical profession, and that's too damned bad. I'm sorry you picked a selfish bastard for a husband, sorry you were hurt, but as far as I'm concerned your experience seems to have been extremely limited. In fact, as far as *I* am concerned, *you don't have any experience at all*." He pulled her closer. "So, until you know what the hell you're talking about, don't——oh, hell!"

And Daniel did what he'd been aching to do all evening. Startled, Edie struggled against him. But Daniel's mouth moved on hers, his lips demanding, coaxing, pleading, and she found herself answering with a demand of her own. And it didn't matter what he had said, or what she had done. Nothing mattered but the moist heat of his mouth taking possession of hers.

"Edie . . . sweet, sweet Edie." He groaned and she could no more resist him than darkness can hold back the morning. Her lips opened hungrily and his kiss captured her. He lifted his hands to clasp her head, fingers sifting through the soft waves, holding her firm beneath the onslaught of his mouth.

The robe slid unnoticed to the floor and Edie's arms reached out to hold him. Shock waves of desire rocked her and she wanted this moment, this sensation, never to end. There was a fire inside her. Daniel had ignited it, perhaps at the very moment she first saw him, and now he kept it burning, spreading, with the movement of his lips—ah, God, like nothing she'd ever known!

Daniel's hands moved over the soft slope of her shoulders under the gown's lacy fabric, and the firm length of her back beneath the silky material. The fragile texture gave him access to every curve, every undulation beneath.

Edie answered with an almost savage response, bewildered at the intensity of her reaction. She trembled uncontrollably, helpless to stem the feverish flood tide pulsing through her body.

Daniel had never felt so powerless. He wanted her: *God help him, he didn't care . . . he wanted her now*. For perhaps the only time in his life he was almost beyond control, making up in one searing instant for a lifetime of direction and restraint.

And Edie was no more able to control her response

to him. Something wild and elemental had broken free within her, had torn loose from the bonds she'd imposed. They were caught together in a blind fury of emotion, swept past the artificial boundaries of caution, unaware of anything but each other.

Daniel's hands slipped over her back, savoring the feel of her body under the softness of the shimmery fabric, branding her skin forever with the remembrance of his touch. His hand stroked her shoulder, pushing aside the delicate straps. The flimsy barrier between them, suspended now only by her breasts, moved with her labored breaths.

She stared up at him, captured by her own passions mirrored in his eyes, scarcely daring to breathe. Desire spiraled at the sight of the hunger etched on Daniel's face. Slowly, so very slowly, his hand slid down, over the sweet, warm skin. She stood almost unmoving, the slight trembling of her body only a fractional sign of her growing arousal.

They were close, so close—only inches separated their bodies, and yet nothing separated them. The very space between joined them together. There was a palpable tension vibrating in the air. Edie waited, breathless, in the circle of his arm, her breasts instinctively pushing into the caress of his fingertips. His gentle hand moved, brushing the hardened crests, and she bit back a moan of pleasure. A fire glowed feverishly in the depths of her golden eyes. Dear heaven, his touch felt so good!

"You feel so good . . ." He whispered her thoughts. "I knew, I knew you'd be like this. I dreamed . . ." He dipped his head and nuzzled her throat. The sweet-clean taste and scent of her, the musky perfume of desire filling him, and the rapid throb of her pulse under his lips echoed in Daniel's heart.

His muttered words, his hands, shook Edie and, but for the support of his embrace, she would have fallen.

Suspended in a glittering web of heated sensuality, she realized neither her years nor her marriage had prepared her for this torrent of emotion Daniel had unleashed. Need for him boiled up inside in an endless fountain of sensation. She almost cried aloud when his hand slipped to her arm: she felt the chill, the emptiness where his touch had warmed her.

Daniel embraced her so tightly she couldn't move, her arms imprisoned under his. And oh, she wanted, *needed* to touch him! But he held her, and then he bent his head, moving his lips along the sweet, sensitive line of her chin, gently nibbling the velvety skin down her throat, arched now in almost total abandon to the wild excitement racing through her blood.

At the touch of his tongue Edie's body went rigid with the tingling anticipation of some incredible revelation. He set her down onto the edge of the bed and knelt before her. Around her breasts he strung a gentle circle of kisses and she knew he could do anything, have anything she could give—as long as he didn't stop this unbearable, exquisite torture!

Ohhh—yes! Daniel's mouth moved moistly across her breasts, his tongue circling first one, then the other. Deep velvet waves of delight washed across her body and in her hunger for more she pulled him closer, closer—

The abrupt sound of a door closing and the distant bark of a dog from somewhere downstairs made for a rude awakening. Like two sleepwalkers, still dazed and uncomprehending, they pulled apart, slowly becoming aware once more of where they were and what they were doing.

Edie's face, flushed with aroused passion, was suddenly drained of color as reality overtook her. The chill air on her bare skin woke her to her state of disarray. Confusion and desire battled for control, and desire fled with the return of reason. She turned from Daniel quickly and slid from the bed, putting distance between them as she hastily fumbled her nightgown back into place and scooped up her robe, trying vainly to hide within its folds.

After a moment Daniel rose stiffly, remorse twisting his features. He tried to speak but his first words were as rusty as an unused hinge. He cleared his throat painfully and tried again. "Edie, I—I don't know what . . . I never planned—"

"Just get out . . . please!" The desperation was there in her words, uttered in a hoarse, intense whisper. She swung around to face him, her eyes glittering in her pale face beneath the tousled hair where his fingers had roamed. "Just leave me alone." Her voice broke but she choked back the sob that threatened to erupt.

"Edie, I know you're . . . upset, but—"

"Upset?" Her teeth were chattering, she was utterly unnerved, her control shattered. Upset!

A spark of impatience flared behind his silvery eyes. "Look, we're both mature adults, we have nothing to be ashamed of. Something incredibly . . . beautiful happened—"

"Nothing happened," she interrupted.

"—beautiful," he went on relentlessly, pushing his fingers through his hair. Daniel managed to steady his breathing. "I don't think we can just forget it happened."

"Well, I intend to. Now get out."

"What the hell are you so afraid of?" Anger, born of frustration and uncertainty, was loud in the harsh question.

Edie, backed into the far corner of the room, sought a refuge that didn't exist for her anymore: Daniel had banished it forever. She had no answer because she couldn't trust him, not yet . . . worse, she couldn't trust herself. The old scars had barely healed. How could she dare chance inflicting new ones?

He turned to go. "I'll call you."

"Don't bother."

"I'll *call*."

She felt trapped, desperate. "Go to hell!"

"Hell?—I've spent most of my life there." Daniel yanked open the door. "I'll call." His words were almost lost with the soft click of the door as he carefully closed it behind him.

Disconsolate, Edie crawled listlessly into her cold bed, throat raw with the effort to hold back tears she refused to shed. She felt crushed under the lonely silence he left behind.

Daniel retreated down the stairs, quiet despair in every step. He pushed past a surprised Lillian, kneeling to unsnap Lorraine's leash just inside the back door. Suddenly aware of his actions, Daniel stopped abruptly.

"Sorry," he mumbled. "I, uh, I'd better be going, it's getting late." Damn, was it too late? "Thanks for . . . everything," he finished lamely. At the door he stopped for a moment, head down, then spun to peer into her kind, startled face.

"That daughter of yours is one miserable, stubborn, pigheaded woman!" Daniel jerked the door closed behind him, the rattling glass resounding in the silence. Then a slow smile crept across Lillian's generous mouth, and looking down at the bored face of the dog, she tapped her finger thoughtfully against her chin.

"See, Lorraine? I just knew they'd be good for each other!"

In the quiet, dark house the shrill ring of the phone struck a jarring note. Edie knew who it was . . . her

A short silence. "My ex-wife is a pretty well-known attorney in Detroit. Very busy, very successful, and very, very dedicated. It's just that she was never quite that dedicated to our marriage." He drew a deep breath and the strangely flat, metallic voice continued. "I suppose that's why she chose to become the ex–Mrs. Slayton." He stopped abruptly. "Oh, what the hell, I should have realized . . . I'm sorry I jumped on you. Of course, if the store is open you have to be there. God! I never thought I was such a male chauvinist. I'll tell you, I don't think I can stand much more self-revelation." His tart words were rife with self-derision. "Well, I'll be seeing you—"

"Wait!" Suddenly Edie knew he mustn't hang up—not yet. Her fears were fighting a losing battle. "Daniel?"

"Uh . . . yes, Edie, what is it?" he asked into the phone, which he now held a good six inches from his numb left ear.

"I, er, I'm really sorry about tomorrow." Silence. A long silence. She sighed. "Well . . ."

"Edie, you did say alternate Sundays, didn't you?"

She sat, hunched over, one hand clutching the receiver in clammy fingers, the other arm hugging her middle, fingers crossed, eyes squeezed shut. Waiting.

"You're not going to make this easy for me, are you?" His rueful laugh came rumbling across the wire. "Ah well, I should have known, considering the progress of our relationship so far."

Our relationship? Is that what we have, a relationship? Edie stared at the phone, heart pounding double-time, the singing of her blood in her ears so loud she completely missed his next words. "Uh, wait, what did you say?" Terrific. She was stammering as if a lead weight were tied to her tongue. Cool, Edie, very cool. He'll really be impressed.

"I asked if you'd come out to lunch next Sunday.

We could even eat from plates, as opposed to my shoes or my lap. No! Wait—don't say it!''

That *might* have been a laugh she heard.

"Sorry," Daniel hurried on. "Forget I said that, all except the part about lunch. Please."

That's all, one quiet word whispered so gently, caressing her ear and sending a tremor of longing skipping across her nervous system.

"If you really want me—" She could have bitten her tongue off the instant the words left her mouth. Perhaps he wouldn't notice.

He noticed. "Oh yes," he said on a wry note, "I want you. How's noon?"

Ha! What would be on the menu besides lunch? "That's fine. Uh, see you next week then, Daniel. And thank you." *I think.* Edie hung up quickly, afraid to listen to the seduction of his voice, thinking of the seven endless days looming ahead.

She slowly made her way upstairs. Shutting the bedroom door, she leaned back, hands clutching the knob, a steady anchor in her shifting universe. At last she pushed away and headed back to bed. A flash of moonlight in the mirror caught her eye.

"Hi there," she whimsically greeted her reflected self, staring into two overly bright eyes flashing back at her. But a pensive expression gradually dampened the eagerness lighting her face. Raising a warning finger, she shook it at the serious image. "And don't you dare come whining and crying if things don't work out the way you want."

The way she wanted. It was the first time she'd actually admitted she was a consenting . . . no, a *willing* partner in this runaway scenario.

Well, of course, any idiot could have told her what she wanted. Him.

* * *

Her last words echoed in Daniel's brain. "Thank you." *No, Edie, I should thank you.* Daniel hung up the phone, still seeing Edie's image as he'd seen her earlier.

Damn, this is ridiculous. Forty-one-year-old men didn't have teenage fantasies. Did they? *God, he must be going crazy.* But it wasn't madness, it was hope, a suddenly radiant sense of expectation and eagerness.

Edie was different, not at all the kind of woman he was used to. Different from Sandra, with her hard-edged intensity to succeed, her cool and deliberate competence in everything she undertook, from the court-room to the bedroom.

By the time he'd reached maturity, perhaps even years earlier, Daniel had been sickened by the shallow sterility of his mother's selfish iron-butterfly existence, her insistence on social form and the importance of a *good name*, and a better bank balance. Her total disregard and incomprehension of other people, their welfare, their lives. Everything was measured by her own insular, narrow yardstick—and usually found wanting. In contrast, Sandra's dedication of purpose had had an almost idealistic purity, an appeal that seemed to be just what he wanted, what he needed, in his life. Too late, he found the two women had more in common than he'd realized.

Daniel had seen, finally, that no matter which direction he tried, he would run headlong into the stern boundary lines of self-interest and passionless insensitivity he'd learned as a child: either the selfishness of personal vanity or the selfishness of professional egoism. There was cold comfort in both, and love and joy in neither.

As one year slid inexorably into another, the quiet despair had grown, until, finally, he labored harder and harder to fill with his work the vacuum left in his life by the absence of any personal bond in family or marriage.

And it hadn't been enough.

The constant pain of the headaches had filled that void when even work had not.

Now, for the first time in a long while, he couldn't wait for tomorrow.

SEVEN

Edie drove slowly, enjoying Michigan's first serious snowflakes, delaying as long as possible her first sight of Daniel's house—and Daniel. Her body alive with tension and sparks of nervous energy, she eased her foot further off the gas pedal.

Coward!

Edie was more than annoyed with herself, a condition becoming much too familiar, and she knew, exactly, the beginning of that dissatisfaction . . . a too memorable Sunday at precisely 4:25 P.M. He'd appeared, and sanity disappeared. Damn! Edie pounded the wheel, frustrated at her indecision where he was concerned. The trouble was, lately he seemed to be concerned *everywhere*.

Everything seemed to remind her somehow of Daniel. She'd sworn to avoid him—made herself a solemn vow. No way would their lives touch again! And one phone call later here she was, headed through sun-glistened snowflakes down this long-familiar road, straight at trouble, and all for the price of a free lunch.

There ain't no free lunch.

On the other hand, there *was* a gut-wrenching sense

of the inevitable. In the fragile serenity of her new life, Daniel Slayton was the nursery rhyme man who wasn't there; Edie was acutely aware when he wasn't there again today. She'd felt it all week: something newly vital was missing. She groaned, the cement mixer at work in her stomach.

I'm not nervous. I am *not nervous*.

Oh Lord, she was so damned nervous.

She scowled. This was just dumb! Outside the car windows, the road unwound relentlessly, a road known and traveled since her childhood. But she was a grown woman now . . . she'd been around, knew the score. He was only a man and this was only a meal.

Edie grinned wryly. Tell it to the Marines, kiddo.

Too soon she turned off the slightly slippery road and covered the distance up the drive to the front of the house. With daylight it was once more the charming, cheerful place it had always been, though now it sparkled with the opulence of restored carpentry and fresh paint. The cold, forbidding personality it projected the last time she'd seen it had disappeared, along with the loneliness and darkness of an autumn night.

Daniel stood in front of the open door, sheltered only a little by the deep overhang of the porch roof that encircled the house. He'd seen her car as it turned in, been waiting for it, though he would not, could not, have admitted it to himself. None of that showed in the carefully impassive face he turned to her, hands thrust into pants pockets against the cold, leaning negligently on one of the pillars framing the steps.

Edie emerged into the scatter of flakes floating lazily from the increasingly overcast sky. The air was cold, with a clear, brittle quality that made her want to inhale deep, gusty breaths, to taste its sharpness, its purity. Impulsively she turned her face upward and opened her mouth, catching a few of the icy crystals on the tip of her tongue.

Daniel's heart lurched for an instant. He watched her walk that last mile, her wariness painfully evident, and let a half-smile emerge. "I must say you look totally underwhelmed."

Actually she looked marvelous, he thought, watching the drifting flakes sparkle jewel-like in her auburn hair. "I promise, my cooking isn't all that bad. And anyway, between us we could come up with an antidote for anything."

What's the antidote for you? Edie climbed the steps, stomach twisting with delicious anticipation. "Well, whatever you've got, if it's hot and ready, I won't complain."

Daniel raised his brows. "Unh-uh, I won't touch that one."

She stopped in mid-step, wide-eyed, face flaming scarlet. "God," she mumbled into the collar of the bright red jacket that now matched her cheeks. "I don't *believe* I said that!" *Blush and shiver, blush and shiver . . . that's all I do lately*, Edie thought in disgust. "I saw a sign once I should have tattooed on my forehead: Do not engage mouth until brain is in gear."

Daniel bit his lips, as close to laughing as he'd been, and she extended the wine bottle she'd been clutching at her side.

"By the way, I brought this, although I guess I should apologize: I'm sure you're a 'cork' person but I'm 'screw-top' all the way—" She stopped abruptly at the inept choice of words. Daniel's smile grew a bit wider and Edie shrugged in cheerful consternation, seriously considering a vow of silence.

"It's just a generic white. If you prefer red, in light of my record so far, perhaps you'd settle for my blood." Laughing, she extended a bared wrist, and Daniel quickly took her hand.

"Truce?" His look was warm with unspoken pleasure.

"Truce!" Edie echoed with a bright sense of relief

and, with his first touch, something else, much more exciting.

"Come on inside, I'm turning blue out here." He guided her through the door and they walked through the spartan elegance of the front hall into what Edie remembered as a cozy, cluttered living room to the left. Daniel held on to her hand.

Edie glanced around, curious, recalling the house from the times she'd played there as a child. Harry Gallatin, the older brother, had been one of her friends and she'd come to many a party and picnic at this house. Daniel watched her face.

"What is it? Something wrong?"

"Oh, no, I—I like what you've done, tearing down the wall between this room and the dining room. It's so bright and airy now and the windows are wonderful! It's almost as if you could forget there's a wall separating us and all that." She made a wide gesture encompassing the stark November beauty beyond the glass.

And she meant it. Gone were the cramped corners and small, crowded rooms she remembered; instead the brightness and lovely variety outside were now part of the room. The best part. Because the rest was cold. Luxurious, expensive, perfect. And *cold*. A model room, and it looked as if no one lived there.

Her silence was not made less uncomfortable by the music drifting from hidden speakers. Edie recognized one of Bach's Brandenburg Concertos, the fifth. Funny, it was one she'd often enjoyed before—but not today, not here. Here it was lifeless, overwhelmed by the relentless, sterile perfection of the room.

"It's . . . impressive, like a picture out of *Architectural Digest*. The decorator did a, uh, a marvelous job." Edie's smile was overbright, her words too quick, and she wasn't entirely successful in repressing her slight shiver of distaste.

White on bloodless white, with here and there a harsh

accent of crystal or black. At the center of the large room, poised before the freestanding stone fireplace, was an unwelcoming huge white sofa. It might have been inspired by the wheeled gurney tables used in hospitals. Floating in lonely isolation on a sea of pristine white carpet, it was flanked by a pair of lucite and silver floor lamps, apparently a pacifier for someone who might actually wish to sit and read. Edie couldn't begin to imagine kicking off her shoes and curling up with a good book on that piece of surgical equipment. Not hardly!

Fronting the sofa a black glass coffee table stood, unadorned save for one exquisite crystal bowl and an artfully placed abstract marble carving. They had been arranged for effect and probably hadn't been moved since. A massive, coldly glittering glass sculpture stood at one side of the window, and its myriad facets reflected faint prisms of refracted light in a cascade of frozen rainbows. A lifeless mockery of the real thing. It was a magnificent object, museum quality, and it fit the set piece of a room to icy perfection. The overall effect was static, lifeless, and if one sought haven or comfort, it was not to be found in this room.

"You don't like it, do you?" As if for the first time, Daniel looked around and tried to see it through her eyes. "Well, I can't say I blame you. Sandra decorated it and I've only just now realized I don't like it much, either. Kind of empty, isn't it?" His words were pensive, bordering on bleak.

"Oh Daniel, no. It's only, well, people have different tastes." Edie prayed she had even a trace of her mother's tact somewhere in her genes—she needed it now! "I'm so used to drowning in a sea of clutter I have a panic attack at the sight of an empty surface. How I *envy* you . . . it must be wonderful to find something any time you want it! I've never gotten the knack." She smiled diffidently. "My mother, as you

may have noticed, is not a great believer in 'a place
for everything—''

"—and everything in its place,' " Daniel finished
her sentence; his sardonic tone, the slight stiffness of
his body, spoke eloquently of the effect of those words.
He let go of her hand.

Damn, Edie thought. *Open mouth, insert foot.*

"Well!" Daniel rubbed his hands together. "I seem
to be a less than perfect host. Why don't I light the fire
and we'll open the wine. We can toast our truce." His
voice was very polite, a bit more distant. It was subtle
but unmistakable.

"Great! I thought it was a little shaky there for a
minute." Edie smiled broadly, silently cursing herself
for almost destroying the fragile bond they'd just begun
to share. *Sometimes, you fool, honesty is not the best
policy. We're building bridges here, remember?*

Daniel moved to the fireplace, set in a rectangular
column of natural fieldstone. The remodeling had
opened it on all sides, and, after the view itself, it was
the nicest, most natural feature of the room. Lord, how
had it escaped Sandra's deadly touch? On an irreverent
impulse Edie hooked her jacket over one of the glittering crystal barbs conveniently protruding from the
"thing" beside the window. She thought it a distinct
improvement.

Edie paused in the act of removing her coat and
watched as Daniel knelt and put a match to the wood
arranged on the grate. The black cashmere sweater
stretched taut across his shoulders as he bent to nurse
the flame to life, and she admired the masculine beauty
of his body.

Not a wasted motion. Every move calculated. And
at any other time Edie would have approved of the taut
precision of his moves. But the rigidity of his posture,
the expression on Daniel's face were at odds with the
man who'd welcomed her so happily only moments

ago. Something had invaded this moment, something cold and unpleasant, and Edie didn't like it. She only knew it had dropped between them like a sheet of ice—they could see, even hear through it, but they were no longer together.

He's so careful! Edie had a sudden, vivid memory of the lonely yet passionate man with whom she'd shared her car one cold night. She longed to see that man again, free of this austere shell in which he seemed trapped. The relentless, rhythmic Bach only emphasized Daniel's own meticulous precision.

He rose, dusting off his hands, and from a cabinet beside the door pulled down two wine goblets, heretofore undesecrated with the likes of Edie's plebeian gift. He unscrewed the cap as if it were a brand-new experience for him.

"Remember, I warned you." Edie shrugged cheerfully, as if she didn't notice anything wrong . . . she refused to let depression share their afternoon. Her performance merited an Oscar.

He handed her a glass and touched his own to it in a silent toast. They sipped, not quite looking at each other, suddenly hesitant, uneasy. Daniel sighed, a life's worth of frustration and dissatisfaction in that small breath. He hadn't anticipated how difficult it would be to turn his life in a different direction from the one he'd followed all these years.

"I'd better check on lunch, I'll be back in a minute. Make yourself at home." The irony of his words was lost on him and he walked quickly from the austere room.

But not, Edie noted wryly, before he carefully took her discarded coat and hung it neatly in the hall closet.

Balanced on the edge of that behemoth of a couch, she felt like Ahab atop Moby Dick, and just as precarious. She had placed this day in a separate, special niche in her dreams; perhaps a new beginning, for her, for both of them, a chance to start over.

How foolish! To become so involved in a dream. How could a mere dream survive a bout with harsh reality?

On the other hand, Edie asked herself, doggedly refusing to just turn her back on the bright promise the afternoon had offered only minutes earlier, there must be some explanation for the sudden chill. She looked around, recalling their conversation before they shared the wine. Oh Lord, of course!

It's really empty, isn't it? Edie heard again that bleak note in his voice. The answer was there, in his own words.

There was more emptiness here than just this room.

She frowned, eyes narrowed in thought. Okay. Her father had taught her if something was important it was damn well worth a fight. Edie was rapidly coming to the conclusion that Daniel might be very important. There was something there . . . something that aroused all sorts of confused feelings. At the very least she would have the chance to find out! No room, no house, *nothing* was going to make her back off now.

Ready or not, Daniel, here I come.

But, she rubbed her hands in unconscious anticipation, first things first. He needed to relax, loosen up, and, by God, Edie Calvin was just the woman to teach him how. She chuckled. Since they'd met, she'd been, *de facto*, a one-woman SWAT team, seeming hell-bent on just that mission.

Recalling their encounters . . . they couldn't be dismissed with so mild a term as "meetings" . . . Edie reflected that he'd become progressively more *relaxed*, and after that scene in her bedroom, if he got any "looser," *she* would probably fall apart. From the awesome effect he had on her mind and body, a latent thread of fear told her she might end up as scrambled as Humpty Dumpty: nothing could ever put her back together again.

Ah, what was the use? That same mind and body had conspired, and the decision, perhaps inevitable from the beginning, had quite obviously been made for her.

Some minutes later Edie resolutely headed for the kitchen. The swinging door was as silent as her stockinged feet and she saw Daniel before he was aware of her. He leaned over the counter, hands braced in front of him, the open prescription vial next to the pan he'd just removed from the oven. Her heart caught in her breast . . . the look on his face was terrible.

His headache again? But what had brought it on so suddenly? *Had she been to blame?*

She almost went to him. But, familiar with her own prickly pride, she knew instinctively he'd feel the same. She retreated back into the hallway as quietly as she'd come.

"Daniel," she called loudly, "anything I can do to help?" Edie pushed open the door. "Oh, there you are. Mmm, smells *great*. Now, if you and that chicken can stop staring at each other for a minute, we can get down to serious business here."

The five-hundred-watt smile on Edie's face lit up the entire kitchen; it did a pretty good job on his spirits, too, Daniel realized. He couldn't possibly prevent his own answering smile and, in that moment, forgot why he'd felt so depressed before she came in.

"Well," he looked back at the dish steaming aromatically on the counter, "I suppose if I have to choose between you . . ." He studied her thoughtfully, "Your legs are much better."

"Some choice!" Edie glanced down at her pants-covered legs. "How can you tell?"

"I figure if they match the rest of you, it's a sure thing." Inexplicably, Daniel shared her exhilaration.

"Of course, we can check out all the parts: legs, thighs—"

"That's far enough, bud." Heat surged through her, leaving a tingling sensation wherever his eyes touched. "Body parts do not belong in the kitchen . . . not my body parts at least. But," she indicated the crusty, glazed bird, "definitely *his*." Oh, it felt right, this bridge they were building . . . friendship. "Let's stick to the stomach—you know, that empty space behind my belt you promised to fill with lunch."

He appraised the area in question. "I'm glad to see it hasn't shrunk beyond repair."

"No need to be insulting," Edie muttered. She recalled, painfully, the ultra-sleek look Mark had preferred and that she'd constantly battled to achieve. Gone now, the same as other reminders of those years. "You are obviously not a gentleman."

"Edie, that was a compliment. I *like* you as is."

Oh, and I like you, *Daniel.* Edie warmed beneath his steady look. With studied nonchalance she nodded toward the medicine by his hand. "Having another of those headaches?"

Daniel looked down at the two tablets in his hand, startled, then slowly replaced them, gratified surprise lighting his eyes. "No. As a matter of fact, I'm not." He put the container of Demerol back into the cupboard and firmly shut the door.

"Hey, that really looks wonderful," a suddenly buoyant Edie gestured at the dish. "May I help?"

"There's a salad in the refrigerator and rolls are in the toaster oven."

"Wow. I'm impressed! You got everything to come out at the same time?" She looked properly awed as she retrieved the food he'd mentioned. He'd set the table in the kitchen but, she saw now, *it* was even more oppressively sterile than the other room had been. Yuck. Not according to plan.

"Daniel, I've got a great idea. Let's have a picnic!"

He stared, as if she had a screw loose, perhaps two, then at the window where snowflakes were still swirling from the leaden sky. "I'm sure you've had better ideas," he said finally.

"Oh, not out there," Edie laughed, "in here." She nodded toward the front of the house.

Daniel looked doubtful. "Well, I've never—"

"Of course you haven't. My point exactly," she muttered, making a face. "But we'll need a tablecloth, or a blanket . . ."

He walked to a door she hadn't noticed before, some kind of utility room, and when he returned, he was holding a bright red blanket. "I hope you don't mind, it's from the hospital's emergency room. I borrowed it to wrap some books and things I brought up here."

"Oh Daniel, it's perfect! It's *beautiful*! Edie took the flame-colored wool and hugged it to her. "It's not white!"

It took a moment and then Daniel began to smile in earnest, suddenly seeing himself through her eyes. He even enjoyed her gentle teasing—a unique experience. Well, actually, *she* was a unique experience. His internal confusion scale registered an eight-plus and was still rising.

Edie was entranced by the beauty of it, pure joy coming to life right there before her eyes, a man who had just discovered a marvelous surprise where none was expected. She almost forgot what they'd been talking about. But she quickly pressed her advantage; who knew how many chances she'd have?

"All right, I'll take these, you get the rest." She disappeared back through the door and he stared after her, bemused, and suddenly chilled by the loneliness she left behind. He hurried to collect the rest of their ersatz picnic and followed her to the living room. And stopped dead in the doorway.

In the short time since he'd left, the room had acquired, miraculously, a kind of vitality, a renascent life that filled the previously arid space. Unerringly his gaze was drawn to the fireplace. The blanket spread on the floor, the serving dishes centered on it, an intense splash of vivid color, illuminated and enlivened the room he knew so well, that he'd never seen before. Edie's red jacket, paroled from the closet, once more hung jauntily on its priceless crystal hook by the window. She had kicked off her shoes, dropping them in careful disarray next to the black ice cube of a table. The casual disorder of coat, shoes, and picnic spelled welcome to his dazed eyes.

Edie had turned off all but one lamp in favor of the muted light of early afternoon and the flaring orange-yellow glow from the blazing logs. The flickering gleam flashed highlights off platters and glasses, off shining copper hair and golden eyes.

Yes, of course, he realized, it was *Edie*, a bright flame of life, the source of warmth and joy. Seeing her there, her capacity for life and color and happiness within his walls, within his life, he realized it suddenly was not so empty or cold anymore. Daniel was stunned; a blinding light had come on in a dark room, and he blinked in the glare of discovery. It was more than a little frightening: there would be no more shadows to hide in.

"You certainly work fast," he observed.

Edie looked up, offering a silent prayer for the rest of the afternoon. "Pull up some floor and sit down." Her breathless voice betrayed the anticipation and eagerness playing havoc with her composure. She marveled at the beautiful fluidity and grace of his movements as he dropped down beside her, depositing the rest of the things in the same supple motion.

He sat, but not quite at ease. Still, Edie convinced herself, she was certain there were untapped reservoirs of humor, of spontaneity, just waiting to be explored. *Christopher Columbus had nothing on me!* She grinned to herself in anticipation. She could hardly wait: she'd better grab some chicken before she grabbed Daniel—she didn't want to scare him off.

My God, what has happened to me in the last few weeks?

"Now, isn't it prettier here in front of the fire?"

"Are you sure," Daniel asked dubiously, "you don't want chairs?" Her look was his answer. "Well, at least knives and forks—oh, all right, all right, I'll try anything once."

She grinned, dropping an eyelid in a conspiratorial wink, and an answering smile flashed in his shining gray eyes, clearer and more unshadowed than she'd yet seen them.

Daniel couldn't remember ever feeling quite this way . . . so strange, so just plain damned good. Whenever he was with Edie, that inner coil of unconscious tension seemed to ease, to unwind, and he found himself relaxing barriers he'd been reinforcing his whole life. On the other hand, when he was with her, when he *thought* about her, the upward progression of his vital signs disclosed a whole spectrum of different tensions straining for relief. Ah, there was tension and then there was *tension*, and this kind he'd learned about at puberty!

He looked at her now, not really hearing her cheerful chatter, just feeling a new sense of completeness. Suddenly aware of his steady gaze, Edie stared back, and her words slowly died away. She heard, as if from some great distance, the melodious backdrop of the music. Bach had given way to Vivaldi and the chill had dissipated. Or was it something else? She tore her eyes away, laughing nervously, unfamiliar with this tremulous new person evolving inside her skin. "Do you think the chicken will take this as a personal rejection?

Maybe we should start to eat.'' Edie grabbed hold of the knife and began to hack away at the unoffending bird. A wince of pain twisted Daniel's smile and he hastily removed the knife from her hand.

"I can't sit by and just watch. At least let me put it out of its misery with some painless surgery. The poor thing didn't do anything to you.''

"Neither did you, but that didn't stop me.''

His mouth spread with a full-fledged, twenty-four-karat, heart-stopping grin. "That's why I have such empathy for poor Chicken Little here. I know how it feels to have the sky fall on you.''

His expression, warm and intimate for that fraction of an instant, enveloped her like a soft caress. She trembled quietly at the imagined touch. Without being aware of her actions, she grabbed a roll from the basket and her shaking fingers began to pull it to shreds. From there, knife-and-forkless, she hurriedly began on the defenseless chicken.

"Edie, sharing meals with you is an excellent way to preserve the silverware,'' Daniel noted dryly, filling his own plate.

"Isn't it a challenge, roughing it this way?'' Her irony was lost on him. Then, as she chewed and swallowed, her eyes opened wide. "Why, Daniel, this is delicious! You did this yourself, without a can opener?'' Her awed, incredulous words were muffled, struggling as they were to emerge from around a mouthful of food.

"I warn you, my repertoire is extremely limited. You've just seen it.'' Daniel's comment was given rather abstractedly. He was holding a chicken leg in his hand, studying it as if he'd never seen one before, the other hand clutching a wad of paper napkins. He tried, as he ate, to forestall the dripping juice from sliding inevitably down his wrist onto his so-far immaculate sweater and crispy clean shirt cuff. It was a silent, grimly fought battle but he was the winner.

"You know, it's absolutely amazing," Daniel said, bemused, looking at the bone in his greasy hand. He gestured at her with it. "In the short time I've known you I've developed this whole new attitude toward food. It used to be just a necessity . . . you know, for survival, maybe an excuse for a social gathering." He studied the messy remains of the meal and diligently removed the evidence from his hands, shaking his head in amused recognition of his metamorphosis. "Since I met you, food has assumed a, shall we say, much more direct, earthy aspect. I've become so personally *involved* with it, a hands-on experience you might say."

"Well, you know what they say: Life is a banquet. I just figure you'd better grab what you can before everything's all gone, or you'll never get to taste anything. You've got to be willing to try something different now and then."

"Is that how you always look at life, expecting it to taste so good? What about the worm in the apple, don't you ever worry about that?"

"Nope," Edie laughed, "I'd only worry about *half* a worm."

"Seriously—"

"That's your trouble, right there, Daniel. You're always too *seriously*."

He sighed in rueful agreement. "But doesn't this 'banquet' ever give you indigestion?" He had the zealous intensity of a disciple learning a newfound religion.

"Daniel, Daniel," Edie shook her head in exasperation. "Why ruin the flavor with pessimistic possibilities? Look, when the bad times come—even as bad as Mark and Sandra," she wrinkled her nose in distaste, "then, they come, and you just manage to live through it. 'This too shall pass' and all that." She looked straight into his thoughtful gray gaze, a challenge in her words. "Why do you always assume the worst? The odds are at least fifty-fifty, after all, and I think they're a lot better than that, in favor of the optimists like me." She thought of a phrase she'd heard from some kids in the drugstore. "Mellow out, Daniel, mellow out!" Her teasing laugh took the sting from her words.

He studied her intently for a moment, then looked down at the remnants of their lunch on the floor beside them. "That's what this is all about. That's why you did this."

Her chuckle trailed off in a tremulous, choking cough. "Did what? Why, Daniel, what are you talking about?"

"Come on, little miss innocent, I'm talking about this, the picnic, the—" he indicated the room, "—everything."

"Well, I don't . . . I mean—" Good God, was this Edie Calvin, golden tongue of the high school debating team, mumbling and stammering as if she'd been caught with her hand in the till? "Oh Edie, you fast-talkin' devil, you!" she muttered.

The merest hint of a smile hovered on Daniel's lips. "Don't be embarrassed, Edie, never with me."

She was suddenly wrapped in the liquid velvet of his quiet gentle words, words that wound themselves around her heart, as his hand wound around hers. She feared she'd never be free of the hold he had on her now.

Free? Before Mark, and since, she'd *been* free, and yet it was only now she felt ready to soar and fly, as she'd never done before Daniel came into her life. So why was she worrying about being free? It was a word, only a word, and now Daniel defined that word. As she somehow knew he would define everything for her from this day on.

"This is the nicest thing anyone's ever done for me." Daniel's voice caught and he had to swallow.

"You know, Edie, I've got a lot of years behind me, a lot of accomplishments, but this is . . . this . . ." He stopped, uncomfortable and hesitant, looking deeply into her shining eyes, her hand warm in his.

"Edie, I'm not an introspective man. Except with my scalpel, I don't probe too deeply. Perhaps I'm afraid of what I'd find. But you, you listen—and you hear the truth I won't face. You see the emptiness I can't admit. And you care enough to fill it." Joy and the quiet wonder of discovery filled his words. Daniel moved his hand, the back of his fingers sliding along her cheek, touching gently the curve of her slightly parted lips. Her soft breath caressed the sensitive pads of his fingers.

Edie leaned toward him, her whole body centered at that instant on their only point of contact, his fingers resting on her mouth. He gently traced the rounded contour, rubbing the soft cushion of her lower lip, the smooth, moist flesh of the inner surface. Gentle shudders trembled along her spine and Edie closed her eyes, concentrating only on the exquisite sensation, the glorious delight of Daniel's touch.

Never, oh *never*, could she have believed how susceptible her body would be to just this slightest brush on her lips, how his light stroke could ignite this tingling thrill. She'd been held, kissed . . . but nothing had ever set her on fire as his merest touch was doing right now. She had the craziest sensation that she *was* soaring, *was* flying . . . floating . . .

A low moan of pleasure bubbled from her throat, and Daniel's own delight rose to an almost unbearable excitement. He ran his thumb along the irregular sharp edge of her teeth. Without thought her tongue touched, tasted, and she closed her lips around him, reveling in the hot, salty tang of his flesh on her, within her. In some far recess of her brain Edie was startled at her own astonishingly intimate response. She was caught up in a voluptuous, irresistible flood of sensation and she needed to explore . . . just a little longer.

Daniel was enthralled, her sweet scent, the sable shadow of lashes resting on pink-tinted cheeks, and he bent to touch his lips to her closed eyelids, to brush feathery lashes. His tongue tasted the dewy moistness on her upper lip, felt the tiny rush of her trembling breath. His body was taut with sudden, straining arousal at this sharing, this small joining.

Edie's breasts rose and fell with each breath and Daniel saw that her body was reacting to him as was his to her. He was awed by the effect she had on him, and more, by the power he seemed to exert over her. Carelessly pushing aside blanket and dishes, he knelt beside her. His hand trembled almost imperceptibly as he brushed the hardened crest of her breasts and he pressed his fingers against the rough wool of her sweater, the sensitive flesh of his palm receptive to the softness, the firmness beneath.

His touch made Edie want more and she pressed greedily into his caress, pushing closer instinctively, knowing here was fulfillment. Excitement built higher, faster, surged through her bloodstream until nothing else existed.

The sudden explosion of desire, this awakening of raw hunger, was stunningly new to Daniel. He couldn't seem to get enough of holding, touching her, seeing how wildly responsive she was under his hands. He'd stumbled on a beautiful new discovery and the leaping pulse of her body told him they'd made the discovery together.

Edie pulled him closer and he groaned, a man in the most exquisite torment. Lips came together in a kiss that was all-devouring need, affirmation, an avowal of hunger and desire, of promise and excitement and wondrous unknown pleasures.

It was an eternity of seconds before they pulled apart,

dragging air into starved lungs, the sound harsh and sibilant in the quiet fall afternoon. Daniel stared unblinking and she could not tear her eyes from the bewildered revelation on his face.

Before today that face had been hard, harsh, carved from the granite of his isolation, almost unrelieved by softness or warmth, a man who didn't hope and didn't dream. But the dream was there, frozen in the ice of his loneliness, waiting. For someone. Someone to bring the sunlight of affection and laughter. It was the face that had, within the instant of her heart's beat, become the single most important thing in Edie Calvin's universe.

"You feel it too, don't you." His hoarse whisper cut through the stillness. It was not a question.

EIGHT

"No!" Like hell she didn't. "No, I . . . I don't know what you mean. It was just a kiss. Let's not make too much of it." Her breathless denial shattered the moment and Edie Calvin, who'd spent a lifetime rushing in ahead of the angels, scrambled out of Daniel's arms and jumped to her feet, ready to run for her life.

Daniel had to exert every ounce of strength to control the feelings that almost overwhelmed him. He sat back on his heels, bracing clawed fingers into taut thighs, then rose stiffly to his feet, unable for a moment to face Edie and the denunciation he would see in her face.

Damn it to hell! I really botched it, didn't I?.

Daniel stood for a moment, hands motionless at his sides. "Sorry," he said stiffly, "I won't force such sloppy sentimentality on you again." He turned and walked to the closet, pulled on a heavy sheepskin jacket, and, without missing a beat, continued out the front door, leaving it swaying back and forth behind him.

Get out fast, he thought. That much, at least, he would do for her. She wouldn't have to face him again;

she could walk out of this house, and his life, and never look back.

Edie stood, staring out the window-wall, listening, ears stubbornly attuned to his every movement. A few seconds later a flicker of motion caught her eye and she saw Daniel stalking away from the house, jacket hanging carelessly open, head bent against random gusts of cold autumn air that dared ruffle his dark hair.

Arms wrapped around her waist, she held herself together with sheer will, her mind and heart trying to understand what had just happened. And something irrevocable had happened. One man's face, one man's touch, one man's kiss. And nothing was the same. Nor would it be again.

Edie, who had never counted cost in her life; who acted on impulse and thought about it later; who wouldn't know the meaning of the word "caution" if Noah Webster shouted it in her ear: fearless Edie Calvin was suddenly deathly afraid of the abyss she saw ahead of her, as bottomless as his smoke-gray eyes, as seductively sweet in its dangerous way as the beautiful mouth that worked such magic; as compelling in its attraction as his strong, gentle hands that held her so sure, so safe, so . . . loved.

No!

That didn't enter into this—it couldn't! What did they know about each other besides this incredible attraction that had drawn them together? But wasn't that exactly what had propelled her into her disastrous marriage to Mark? Hadn't she thought she loved him, too? Obviously judgment was not her strong point, so how could she trust herself again? She'd almost fallen—well no, let's be honest, her feverish mind insisted—*thrown* herself into the arms of a stranger. An exciting, desirable, heart-stopping stranger who touched a chord in her soul never struck before, but a stranger nonetheless. Edie made a vain effort to regain her equilibrium, slow her racing pulse.

Could it happen this way? Is this what it was like? Love? No, not this fast. Of course not. But why not? she wondered. And, if not yet, then she feared she was well on the way, maybe past the point of no return.

Edie looked after Daniel's receding figure, growing fainter with distance and the lowering haze of the cloudy afternoon. If she were smart, she'd run—as far and as fast as she could before he did more damage to her so newly reclaimed independence and self-respect. Mark had bruised her heart—*and worse, she ruefully admitted, her ego*. But Daniel! Dear Lord, if she let him, he'd completely destroy her. Already she felt as if she'd been on the losing end of a collision with a Mack truck. After one kiss! *Oh no, for once in your life, Edith Stephanie Calvin, discretion is definitely going to be the better part of valor.*

With a decisive nod she put her shoes on, grabbed her coat from its crystal perch, and, by now almost running, flung herself through the open door, banging its bright brass knocker against the shiny black enameled wood panel. She thought fleetingly how very unstrung Daniel must be: his hair was messed and he'd left the door open. *The mind boggles.*

Intent on escape, Edie reached her car and stood for a long moment, staring down at her hand. Then, straightening her shoulders, she turned and followed Daniel's path through the trees. Breathless, frightened at the enormity of her capitulation—so sudden, so complete—she came, at last, to where he stood on the brittle brown grass beside the dark, turbulent lake.

Feet planted in go-to-hell defiance, he stood ramrod stiff, visibly pulling strength back around him like a battered shield. But stark lines of pain were etched across his stony face. He held himself with an unnatural, unyielding rigidity. Her first impression was of tightly leashed fury. And then, instinctively, her insight went far beyond what she saw.

Not anger, but the habitually self-protective posture of a man steeled against possible danger and probable injury. A man who would not easily allow anyone to see the doubts, the vulnerability beneath the aloof assurance he presented to the world.

But—he had allowed *her* a glimpse of the man hidden inside, the warmth, the gentleness. A man searching. He'd exposed that part of himself to her, taken the very real chance of being hurt. The initial relief Edie felt on once more taking charge of her own body and soul faded in the sudden white-hot light of revelation. Seeing him, the toll this afternoon had taken, his characteristic self-control, his innate caution now scattered to the winds, she saw clearly just what this day had meant.

"Daniel?"

The word roused him and, so quickly she had to blink, he was once more the hard, cool, protected man she'd first known. A sardonic smile, which was not really a smile, twisted his mouth.

"Still here? I thought you'd be halfway home by now."

"Yeah, that would be the sensible thing to do. Probably why I'm not." Her smile was enigmatic. "Actually, I think it was the front door that did it." He stared at her, frowning. "Don't worry, someday I'll explain. Anyway, it's not polite to eat and run." She looked into his eyes and pressed his cold hand to her lips. "I don't want to run . . . not from you, Daniel."

He stared down at her with that shuttered gray barrier in his eyes, the expression she'd come to know too well. Whatever he saw must have convinced him of what he so desperately wanted to believe. Edie could see the faint ember of hope begin to dissolve that hated icy resolve of his.

With profound gratitude to whatever good angel had granted him this reprieve, Daniel pulled her to him, gathering her close, unable to give voice to the feelings churning inside him. Their bodies beneath the open jackets merged in a shared heat. They were swept up in a myriad of sensations, caring and tenderness and a thousand nameless, wondrous emotions, pledges and promises still to be explored, memories yet to be.

Edie held him, arms twined around his solid frame, feeling the potent force of his strength under her hands, aware of the dormant power that needed only the right catalyst to set it free.

She nestled her head closer, where it rested on the broad expanse of his chest, comforted in the shelter of his arms. The steady heartbeat under her cheek punctuated the eager rush of reassurance and optimism deepening around them.

Daniel smoothed back her hair and he was content, just then, merely to bask in the warmth of their embrace, the promise it held. He could wait. "It's been pretty fast," he murmured, his words caught in the copper tangle of her wind-whipped .... he moved his lips caressingly across the sweet, shiny mass, loving the feel of it on his mouth, the scent, the taste, all blending with the crisp fall air and a faint whiff of wood smoke. "I wasn't prepared for it. This," he hugged her possessively, fiercely, "it's a whole new experience for me. I feel as if I've just discovered fire and I'm not quite sure what to do with it." He might get burned but, oh God, the heat felt so wonderful!

Poor Daniel. Edie shook her head in rueful acknowledgment. He, so much more than even she, had been tossed into a situation he couldn't know, caught in a whirlpool of sensations and reaction he didn't understand, at war with himself and with neither weapons nor protection. *Although his weapons are sure potent against my feeble defenses!*

Edie leaned back in the circle of his arms and slid her hands up to his shoulders, then clasped them behind his neck. She could feel the lingering tension, see it moving behind his pewter gaze. Her fingers massaged, stroking the skin, the taut tendons, then upward, pushing luxuriously through the thick hair, pressing firmly across the contours of his head. For her it was as instinctive as the movement of air in and out of her lungs. How she loved the feel of him!

"Y'know, we're in big trouble, Daniel. Ironic, isn't it? For once, you weren't careful enough . . . and me, for the first time in my life, I'm checking out every step I take." She was trapped in the smoky intensity of his serious eyes. "Cheer up, Daniel, it only hurts for a while—or so I've heard." *Lord, I hope so!*

Cupping his wind-reddened cheeks in her small hands, her thumbs lovingly traced the sharp ridge of his cheekbones and down across the lips that raised her boiling point way beyond all rational limits. Her smile dissipated any chill he might be suffering. For her part Edie was thoroughly warmed by the soft radiance in the gray depths of his eyes, his slow answering smile.

"Uh, Daniel . . . ?"

"Mmmmm?"

"The blood in my toes is beginning to solidify, and I think my nose is about to fall off."

"You're cold?" His eyebrows rose in concern.

"No, of course not, my lips look good in blue." Edie snuggled closer. "Now you, on the other hand, feel nice and warm."

"The nurses in the hospital have a joke, pretty bad, but appropriate." His voice dropped to a throaty whisper and he cradled her tightly against his body, effectively demonstrating exactly where the source of that warmth could be found. "Right now they'd probably describe me as a Bugs Bunny."

She stared, waiting for him to explain.

"What's up, Doc?"

She closed her eyes and groaned. "You're right, it's a pretty bad joke. That's some raunchy bunch of nurses you've got there, Daniel." Suddenly Edie's eyes opened wide and her mouth fell open with amazed delight. She pulled back, laughing. "Why Daniel—it *was* a joke. It was definitely a joke!"

"Well, not so bad for a rank amateur!" he said, moving to draw her back to him. She held up her hand.

"Hold it, buster. I think we'd better take a little walk. I need to warm up, and you *definitely* need to cool down. And we both need to talk."

"Coward." But he nodded, smiling, and they moved toward the frost-bound shoreline ahead of them. Amid the now diminished sprinkle of flakes they stepped onto the damp sand and began to tramp the length of deserted beach, careful to maintain distance between bodies very much aware of each other. They each sensed the need for this short interim of neutrality and by unspoken mutual consent kept the conversation on impersonal grounds.

Daniel found himself fascinated by Edie's reminiscences of growing up in the small town, a life of involvement and intimacy that was a refreshing discovery for him.

"I wish I'd known you then."

"Oh, I don't think you'd have been terribly fond of me, Daniel," Edie grimaced. "Under the carrot-top and the baby fat was a tomboy, nuisance, pest—choose one or all of the above. Oh yes, I struck terror in innocent hearts. Just ask Ronnie!"

"Who's Ronnie?" Daniel asked, then smiled. "No, don't tell me: Lorraine's brother?"

Edie grinned, shaking her fist in his direction. "You're a hard man, Daniel Slayton. Can't you forgive and forget?"

"Hell, if I played rotten tricks like that, I'd want to

forget them, too.'' He laughed heartily. God, it felt good!

"Hey, what happened to our truce? What do you want, unconditional surrender?"

"Well, of course. That's what we both want." Their eyes held for a moment, exchanging wordless promises.

"So, anyway, who's Ronnie?"

"Ronnie Kinsella, my cousin, my mother's sister's son." She looked back with relish at those early years. "Lord, I can't count the Saturday afternoons I tormented him. My mother and Aunt Essie absolutely *forced* him to take me to the movies. Poor thing, he always had to drag me along with his friends." She shook her head in wry amusement. "But did he get even! He kept taking me to horror movies and he wouldn't let me close my eyes in the scary parts, the wretch! He thought I'd finally stay home—but I *loved* them, the more horror the better. Poor Ronnie, *I* was more horrible than Godzilla or the Blob ever was!"

"Well, he shouldn't complain." Daniel, smiling faintly, jammed his hands into his pants pockets. "He had you and Godzilla too. Of course, I've never seen him but Godzilla couldn't have been as pretty or as much fun as you."

Something in his voice made her turn. "What do you mean? Daniel, didn't you go to the show when you were a kid?" It never occurred to her that any child with two coins to rub together could have missed the tribal rite of the Saturday kiddie matinee.

He shook his head once, an abrupt denial. "No. I believe the word my mother used when I asked was 'vulgar,' or maybe it was 'tasteless.' " Daniel shrugged and, tilting his head, gazed at her thoughtfully. "You truly enjoyed your childhood, didn't you?" he asked, sounding faintly curious, then turned and stared out at the restless lake. The waters tossed aimlessly, currents shifting, fluctuating, disturbed by the invisible ferment beneath the surface, the chill breeze above. A pale imitation of his own state, he thought. "Mine was an endurance contest."

Edie felt an ineffable sadness at the picture his dispassionate matter-of-fact words conveyed. All she could do was wait for him to go on.

"I want to thank you, Edie." She looked at him, puzzled. "Last week, that dinner at your house—lukewarm pizza, paper plates, and all—was one of the nicest times I've had. In fact, the whole evening was . . . memorable." For a moment he smiled, remembering. "You know, Edie, your mother is a beautiful woman."

"Why, thank you, Daniel." Edie was totally perplexed at the apparent shift in his thoughts. "I dearly love her but I guess I've never thought of her as particularly *beautiful*. Cute maybe, but after all, the hair's more than a little gray and there are the wrinkles—excuse me, laugh lines!—and she's a bit *chubby* shall we say? But I suppose, like Band-Aids and brownies, that all comes with the territory." She grinned up at him—and froze at the sudden opaque steel of his eyes.

"Oh no, Edie, that's where you're dead wrong. There *are* mothers who have never set foot on that particular territory."

Edie felt a deeper chill than the autumn wind could cause.

"You know," he mused, "all those years I don't ever recall hearing laughter in that house. I suppose there really wasn't much to laugh about. That was *my* mother's territory."

Daniel bent to pick up a handful of pebbles, hefting them absently in his hands, then aiming them one by one across the choppy wavelets, his words punctuating forcefully the staccato splashing of the stones. "One must—*always*—conduct oneself with *propriety*. We—have certain—*standards*. What will people—*think*. Oh, we were big on *standards* and *appearances*."

His back was partly turned and the harsh irony blew back to her on cold gusts of air, the words coming progressively faster, hurrying to break free at last. "Of course, *fun* wasn't part of the approved vocabulary, but then neither was *love*."

Edie's quiet words cut through the silent void. "Is that how you learned about 'sloppy sentimentality'?" She moved closer, and though she ached to put her arms around him, to feel his warmth and strength, to give him hers, she instinctively held back, sensing that he needed to purge himself of the corrosive bitterness before he could accept any comfort she might offer. It was very important she understand the child now that she was so close to loving the man.

"Oh yes, I learned it at my mother's knee, so to speak. Figuratively, of course." Daniel stared down at the indistinct ragged line where land and water merged and pulled apart in their endlessly shifting rhythms, searching for words in the restless pattern of lacy spume washing over the sand.

"She was quite a beauty. Still is." His voice was hard, flat. "Diamonds are beautiful, too. Of course, you can't hold them too close, they're sharp and cold, and hard—hardest things in the world, you know. They can cut anything. On the other hand, they don't offer much in the way of comfort or warmth, or affection. They can't give it and they damn well don't inspire it." His words followed in an inexorable procession. "There's a profound truth there, somewhere: a show-place isn't necessarily a home, and a woman who gives birth isn't always a mother."

The sudden silence was terrible. "You haven't mentioned your father." Edie had an awful need to know it all. As he surely needed, finally, to tell it.

"I was only seven when he died; I was probably the only one who mourned him at all." Daniel shrugged slightly. "He was a quiet man, a pale gray ghost always in my mother's shadow. But at least *he* seemed to enjoy having a child. It certainly wasn't a match made in heaven . . . more likely some corporate boardroom. He had the name, but *she* had the money, *lots and lots* of money. No one was ever allowed to forget it, least of all him.''

"Stop that, Daniel." Edie's voice was quiet, hiding her concern and anger for the years stolen from him. Years that for her had been joyous and for him had held only the sterile emptiness she'd heard in his words. The emptiness that was eating away at him still. Her heart ached with the need to fill it. More, she was just plain angry! "You're a wonderful man, with so much to . . . to . . . Listen, you've wasted enough time! No matter what she's worth, she isn't worth *one more minute of your life*!''

He stared at her. "She *isn't* part of my life, not for years. And I've certainly never been part of hers, not as far as she could help. Oh, we see each other now and then, and we're certainly *polite*, but that's as far as it goes.'' His mouth turned up in an ugly smile. "That's the way we both want it.''

Suddenly Daniel shook his head, a sharp, angry gesture. His mouth twisted in self-annoyance. "But you're right. That, dear friends, ends today's sad, sad story.'' He was patently disgusted with his weakness. "My God, I don't know why I dredged up all that garbage, it was years ago!''

He straightened his shoulders and, with visible effort, turned away from corrosive memories. With a weak smile he turned to Edie. "Come on, let's get moving or we'll be here until the spring thaw.''

She smiled back and began to walk on until sudden comprehension jerked her back from the boundaries of compassion, and she impaled him with a challenging stare. "You! You're . . . rich! I mean, *really rich!* Aren't you!''

Her abrupt accusation startled him out of the last of his bitter reverie. "Yes," he said, puzzled. "You could even say filthy. Why?"

Edie looked unhappy, that disclosure as distasteful to her as his previous words had been.

"There's nothing inherently wrong with money, Edie. It's not a social disease." There was an acid amusement in his voice. "Some of my best friends are rich."

Edie couldn't repress the sneer. It was a conditioned response to the perceived analogy between "rich" and "doctor" that was instantly branded on her brain.

"What's wrong, was your husband rich?"

"No, but he sure wanted to be! And he didn't let *anything* or *anyone* stand in his way!"

Edie spun away to stare blindly across the water, aware of the ugliness of her quick judgments. She was too honest to ignore the truth. "Oh hell, I'm sorry. You're right to be annoyed, Daniel. I guess I've got my head screwed on backwards; I just keep looking at the past. The fact that Mark was screwing half a dozen of his rich patients, and tossed me out when one of them became permanently available, isn't your fault." She looked at him finally and shook her head. "Funny, isn't it? Your mother and I seem to have something in common: a terrible preoccupation with money."

"Edie, don't even put yourself in the same sentence with her." He took a step toward her. "Anyway, to quote, he's not worth one more minute of your life. That was then, this is *now*." He laughed at the irony of his own words. "That's something, it seems, we both have to learn." He watched her intently, then smiled as if a decision had been made at last. "The hell with yesterday. Let's concentrate on now. I think we're both due for an about-face." He took her hand and her answering grin warmed the frigid afternoon.

They made their way back over the wet sand, hands

clasped tightly, bodies so close now Edie felt, with each step, the brush of his hip, his thigh. Every movement, every touch, was a warm, intimate token of the excitement Daniel's body lit in hers, the constant heated pressure of their joined hands an exhilarating reminder of the growing bond between them. She took a deep breath of cold, moist air, more content at that moment than she'd been in a very long time.

"Gee, Daniel, I haven't been out here for—I don't even remember how long it's been!" She looked around and smiled with unrestrained exuberance. "We had such great times on this lake . . . swimming, playing on the beach, ice-skating in winter, sand castles in summer. How I used to love the feel of wet sand squishing between my toes!" She noted his skeptical smile as he listened, watching her. "Don't you love to walk barefoot in the sand? Damn, if it weren't so cold . . . well, maybe next summer we'll—!"

She wanted to share with him, with the entire universe, her supreme joy in the happiness of that golden moment. A radiantly smiling Edie whirled to face him, arms stretched in a spontaneous gesture. She regretted *that* thoughtless little impulse almost immediately.

Edie's arms flew wide and Daniel stepped back quickly to avoid a right to the chin—his foot tangled with a twisted branch of driftwood washed up on shore—he stumbled, trying to keep his balance—

Oh God, she thought horrified, *so that's what they mean by the domino effect.*

Daniel looked down in dismay and stared in growing incredulity. So did Edie. They saw the icy water churn around his feet, foam swirl daintily around his ankles, and his shoes disappear beneath the clinging liquefied sand of the mucky shoreline.

"The peaceful country life isn't all it's cracked up to be." His quiet drawl was deceptive, barely concealing a latent intent under the seemingly casual words. "At least for some of us." He took a firm grip on her arm and, in enforced proximity, they stood mesmerized, for what only seemed an eternity, staring down in curious disbelief and, for at least one of them, sheer dread.

Suddenly Edie felt herself literally dragged up on the beach, her feet barely skimming the ground. Daniel headed for the house, pulling her in his wake as single-minded and effortless as an ocean liner hauling a rowboat.

"Wait, Daniel," she gasped, trying desperately to match his longer stride. "Wait. Stop!" She might as well yell at a tree. Distracted thoughts and images flashed through her numbed brain. Damn, had she walked under a ladder? Broken a mirror? Had *he* broken a mirror? Whatever! She was history, she *knew* it. And not a court in the country would convict him. Even *she* couldn't blame him!

By then he was propelling her into the house, slamming the door behind them. Edie would have been grateful for the comforting warmth, if she'd noticed it. She stared fixedly at the ceiling, the wall, the floor—anywhere but Daniel, who deposited her next to the couch in front of the now low-burning fire. He quickly added more wood.

Her low mumble was almost inaudible.

"What?" He stared at her, inclining his head as if he didn't want to chance missing a single word.

She squeezed her eyes shut, muttering, "I, Edith Stephanie Calvin, being of sound mind—"

"Debatable."

Edie, *in extremis*, didn't even notice his interruption.

"Sit." His tone dared her to argue.

She sat.

"I want to show you something, an interesting little collection of mine. A kind of hobby, I guess you'd call it." The sudden, sweet reason of his voice was even more ominous than anger. "It's changed my life, and I want to share it with you."

She stared at him as if he'd suddenly lost his mind.

Daniel sloshed to the cupboard near the window and, opening the lower door, leaned down to remove the contents.

Edie's eyes narrowed in confusion and she stared, bewildered, at the bundle he handled with such tender devotion. And then the random assortment of motley rags assumed an unforgettable, painful familiarity.

"You . . . you have a garbage fettish?" she asked faintly.

Daniel's only answer was silence and a warning frown—a chilling sight given Edie's state of mind. He held up his assorted treasures with a flourish, like a magician demonstrating the fine art of sleight of hand, and tossed them dramatically, one by one, onto the couch where she huddled in deepening dismay.

Carefully preserved in their recently acquired state of ruined glory were a gray down jacket, mottled now with dark green globs that a privileged two knew to be shampoo; black corduroy pants that had shared the same fate; a pair of stained and torn khaki twill pants, what was left of them; and two black leather shoes, one of which was coated with a repulsive-looking scummy substance that had once been French vanilla ice cream. The most recent addition was a tomato-stained ensemble, shirt and pants, which Edie immediately recognized as cheese-and-everything-hold-the-anchovies.

"You saved all this . . . just for me?" she croaked. "Oh Daniel, you shouldn't have."

He interrupted the removal of his sweater with a raised-brow glance aimed right between her eyes.

Now, as the pièce de résistance of his impromptu performance, Daniel proceeded to remove his water-logged hand-sewn suede loafers. He held them aloft, then slowly turned them upside down, watching as a stream of water and sand cascaded onto the picnic-littered red blanket. Ceremoniously he added them to the small mountain of incriminating evidence.

"You were right," he murmured thoughtfully. "There is definitely something unforgettable about 'squishing' sand between your toes."

Edie looked away, wondering dazedly what a nice girl like her was doing in a place like this. She jumped at the harsh sound of ripping fabric.

"Wh-what . . . what are you *doing*?" Her voice squealed uncontrollably on the last word and she sat tense, hands clenched over perspiration-slick palms, crouched on the edge of the couch. She felt very much at his mercy as he towered above her, deliberately and methodically tearing in half his expensive silk shirt.

"Are you crazy?"

"Yes, I guess I am crazy! You're *making* me crazy!" Suddenly he grinned, a rather wolfish grin she thought. "You've been making me crazy since I first set eyes on you. I was perfectly sane—stuffy, maybe, but *sane*—until you began using me as a—a . . . a drop-cloth for all the assorted garbage you toss around." He dropped the tattered silk to the floor and stepped over it, toward her. She shivered.

"Well, all right." The ominous smile widened and then—he winked! "If you can't beat 'em, join 'em. You've gone to so much trouble to relieve me of my clothes—you've destroyed a major part of my ward-robe!—I'm going to help you get rid of the rest of them." His expression softened and his voice dropped to a gentle whisper.

"Isn't that what you want? Isn't that what we both want?"

NINE

The shadows quivered with the challenge, the stillness broken only by the sudden crackle of burning wood and an answering shower of golden sparks. The dazed look in her eyes locked him in a visual embrace as intense as any physical hold would be.

What you want. What you want. It echoed, spinning through Edie's mind, a truth she'd known forever.

Slowly she unclenched her fingers, her body strangely languid now, and with a shaky breath rose to her feet. Beneath the surface calm a heavy intoxication moved in her blood; her eyes were fixed on Daniel. After her vaguely imagined fantasies his body was a beautiful reality. For a moment more she watched him, the flickering firelight gilding his bare torso. The flames ebbed and flared fitfully, the play of light and shadow enunciating in a random display the unique beauty of his masculinity. Fire shine danced in loving progression over smooth skin, luminous as dull bronze in the suffused light. A shimmering glow caressed his form, darting here and there like a fickle lover, unable to settle on any one aspect because all were so equally desirable. The sharp angle of his collarbone, shadowing the pulsing hollow at the base of his neck, the powerful line of the shoulder as it flowed into muscular arms, more pronounced now as they remained flexed, tense, hands gripping the glimmering silver buckle of his open belt.

For one bright moment the flare of light picked out the line of his bent arms, a dusting of dark hair skimming the taut muscles. A statue, all shadow and flame, embodying strength and stability, he was a steady anchor in the chaos of her senses.

Blind instinct took command of reason. Edie's coat dropped to the floor and she moved, avoiding the clutter at her feet without conscious thought, unable and unwilling to resist the relentless bond that drew her to him. Daniel slowly raised his hand, not quite touching her, and she swayed toward him. Still inches apart, still silent, each looked with hunger into eyes that returned the same message.

Slowly she lifted her hand and laid it on his arm, the solid muscle warm and firm under her fingers. Then, because she seemed to have no options left, she slid her hands up over his shoulders and held his face between her hands. That touch . . . ah, it wasn't, couldn't be, enough. In one fluid motion Edie pulled her sweater up and over her head, dropping it to the floor.

"Daniel . . ." Edie's husky whisper broke the swollen silence. "Please, Daniel, hold me."

Daniel caught his breath and felt as if his heart would crack open. At last he touched her, skimming his fingers over the soft, bare curve of her arms.

A hot starburst of sensation, sudden and intense, played havoc with Edie's nervous system. A small, still voice whispered somewhere in her mind, mocking resolutions, promises, sacred vows made in the cold light of reason. What meaning had they in the face of this vibrant explosion of feeling.

His fingers, tentative at first, brushed across her breasts, taut and aroused beneath their lacy restraint.

He pulled her roughly into an embrace that felt like bands of steel to Edie. Then, more possessively, his hands moved across her back, caressing the ridges of her spine, quickly discarding the fragile barrier of her bra.

Shifting slightly, Edie pulled away just enough to let it slide to the floor, and he held her close again in his arms. The sensation of skin on skin, firm and soft, touching, sliding, strained control to the breaking point. With shaking fingers, caught in the almost trancelike state of suspension, he gently stroked the smooth, glowing flesh of her shoulders, her arms.

The slightest touch and Edie's body gave itself over to Daniel's loving hands. She wanted nothing so much as to feel, to revel in, the wonder of his touch. Her involuntary whimper of unspoken need shattered the fragile unreality, leaving Daniel more shaken than he'd ever been in his life.

He moved his hands up through her hair, holding her head firmly. Looking deeply into her eyes, Daniel lowered his mouth with the unmistakable right of a lord laying claim to his domain. And Edie surrendered gratefully, her feverish response welling up from depths she hadn't dreamt she possessed. Mouths open, hungry for each other, they strained to pull even closer, to snap the unbearable net of tension in which they were caught.

Moments later he held her away, looking with slightly glazed eyes at her flushed face shining up at him with a glorious glowing radiance. The diffused light of the fire shine bathed her skin in a golden pink glow, the tips of her breasts a deeper velvety coral. Impatient, he bent to taste the sweetness she offered. His tongue laved the rigid peaks, teeth and lips drawing her into the heat and passion of his mouth. She sighed, in desperate need of him.

Silent, still in the grip of a special magic, Daniel

stepped back, curled her into his arm, and, without needing to speak, they walked to the stairs; her face was alight with an intriguing mixture of sensuality and contentment. They left behind the warmth of the ebbing flames, generating another, more intense heat of their own.

The bedroom was dim, the light of late afternoon barely filtering through the drawn draperies. It wrapped them in a timeless mood of suspended reality, a feeling that they, and the room, were not of this world, or even this dimension.

Her own quick, shallow breath was all Edie could hear at first. Strangely light-headed, she realized the surge of muted thunder in her ears, drowning out all else, was the torrent of her pulse, pounding feverishly through her veins.

And even that faded as they came together in the seductive choreography of desire. Endless seconds later, the last scrap of their clothing fell away. Exultant, Edie slipped her arms around Daniel's neck, needing to bring him closer, ever closer, to fill the painful void that throbbed achingly deep inside her.

Daniel slid his hands over her waist and down to cup her hips, pulling her to him with the same savage need she was feeling, an urgency she knew was so strange, so new to him. The hard thrust of him into her softness was an imperative allusion to what would, what *must* be. He lowered her, then followed, down to the smooth, soft velvet of the spread, facing her, his hand moving lovingly along the upthrust curve of her hip.

And then his lips covered her mouth again, and the fire inside her loins flared to life again, and the world shifted crazily again.

Dear God, how I love him.

This awesome revelation burst with the brilliance of a kaleidoscope. *Love him!* Her fingers dug into his arms, his shoulders, as the force of her response swept over her, consuming all other thoughts except the delirious excitement they shared and the exquisite joy of her sudden discovery.

"I've dreamed this . . . wanted . . . oh God, Edie, I didn't even know until now how much! I'm burning, and you're the fire."

She gasped as he moved his hand across the soft roundness of her stomach, the subtle swell of ribs, the shifting curve of her breasts. His touch was as light, as gentle as the puff of his warm breath on the sensitive curve of her ear. He nibbled tenderly on the soft, fleshy lobe, strung a line of kisses over her jaw and down her neck, nuzzling the soft arc of her shoulder. With the moist tip of his tongue he tasted the sweet, musky scent of her skin. The double assault shredded the last of her fragile control and her body trembled under his hands.

"Ahhh, Daniel . . . so good, so g . . ." Her breathless murmurings fluttered in the dusk as her hands found their way to his dark head, bent over her breast. He suckled the tender peaks and she held him there, lost in the delicious sensations.

He shifted slightly and she moaned, the loneliness of her body a painful thing until he touched her mouth once more with his lips. With the sweet aggression of his kiss Edie found herself slipping, forever, into a new and different world—Daniel's world.

"Now—please, Daniel. Now! I . . . I can't . . . oh, yessss . . ."

His caresses skimmed, stroked, hovered on the soft nest of russet curls between her thighs. He, too, was almost beyond control and yet he tried to hold back, some part of him needing just as much to know more of that wild sensuality of her reaction, the eagerness, the unfeigned ardor of her hunger for him. His firm, gentle fingers stroked the velvet flesh, moist and hot, and Daniel was lost in the wonder of Edie's response to his touch.

A racking series of shivery tremors exploded deep within her, flooding up through her body and rushing out to every part of her. Toes, fingers, the surface of her skin tingled with a force unmatched by anything she'd ever known. Exquisite tiny convulsions shuddered through her, wave after wave, with a radiant, pulsing throb reverberating all along her body.

"Oh God, it's . . . it's so . . . don't stop . . . ahhh!" The strangled moan that broke free of her parted lips reached down inside him and curled itself around his heart. That he had shared this moment with her, that *he* had given her this! Daniel had never believed there was anything in him that could inspire this kind of response from a woman. But then he had never known a woman like Edie Calvin.

She had opened herself to him, in all ways, held nothing back. An indescribable, unknown tenderness welled up within him, an innate part now of the arousal his body was still experiencing. The depths of her vibrant rapture had unlocked a driving force in Daniel that had not yet been satisfied. He wondered, fleetingly, if it would ever be completely satisfied.

Edie lay quiet in Daniel's arms for a few moments, drained. He continued to stroke her, her breath steadying and slowing, still in the throes of the dazzling riot of revelations she'd made about herself.

"And I thought I knew all there is to know about me," she murmured when she could finally form a coherent thought. "I never . . . I can't believe . . ." She sighed deeply. "Wow, Daniel, what just happened? I mean, I *know* what happened, but how—? Oh hell, I know *how*, too." Her smile was beatific. "That . . . God, that was unbelievable!"

As if flesh had dissolved, leaving all the delicate intricacies of her nervous system utterly exposed, every slightest touch of Daniel's, even a gentle kiss, a breath, was a stimulus sending a thousand wild tremors quaking across her body, a body independent of rational thought, a body now attuned only to him, and would be, always.

The delicious fire in her body, smoldering, flared again. With his relentless caresses Daniel aroused erotic zones she didn't even know existed, and Daniel, who jealousy guarded his emotions, as stingy as Scrooge with his pennies, felt his heart break loose from bonds formed through an endless lifetime. He indulged this newly discovered pleasure in pleasure, this desire for desire—and their joyous intimacies became an intoxicant, overpowering in its effect on a man who had never been exposed to it before.

"Edie," he groaned, his voice thick with desire, "I . . . I need you so much!" She smoothed back his hair, held his lean face between her hands, and pulled him down to kiss her even as she arched up to meet him.

He thrust into her and she absorbed him, not as the first time, but as if they were now *reunited* at last. Edie thought she must be delirious with the shattering sensations jolting through her. She shut her eyes, trying to contain and prolong this glowing, shimmering fantasy, this hidden world they'd found, filled with fiery joy and lights and dazzling whirls of color. . . .

The room, dark now and quiet, enfolded them in its serenity, as they enfolded each other, fused in a loving embrace neither was capable of breaking. Daniel pulled the thick spread over them and only the gentle susurration of muffled sighs, soft murmurs of pleasure and contentment, disturbed the quiet air of what had become, at least for a while, their demi-paradise.

"Wow!" Edie's softly purred exclamation was filled with wonder.

Daniel slid from atop her sweetly quiescent body, carefully pulling her into the crook of his arm, nestling her firmly next to him. Edie burrowed blindly into the warmth and shelter he offered, moving her swollen mouth across the smooth expanse of his broad chest.

"Mmm . . . when you serve lunch—! Where did you learn to cook like that?" She felt Daniel's chuckle reverberate in his chest. "I think you've just made restaurants obsolete. *This* is definitely the place to be!"

"Well, it's certainly the safest—at least this way I don't have to worry about losing any more clothes. Hey, now, you see? I knew we'd come up with a solution to that problem." Laughing, he reached for the bedside lamp, switching it on to a dim light; she blinked and snuggled closer.

"In fact, when I'm with you, I think I may just dispense with clothing completely." Daniel smiled contentedly in happy contemplation of the thought.

"Mmm, how come I didn't think of that?" Edie purred.

"I thought you did. Isn't that what started all this?"

"Now, Daniel, I don't recall doing a solo! I did have some help along the way." She grinned and he placed a kiss on the tip of her nose, then bit it gently.

"Don't get so uppity, young lady! Nobody likes a smart-ass. Although, in your case . . ." His hands, beneath the cover, glided down her body to lovingly fondle the area in question.

They lay in a lovers' embrace, legs entwined, and she rubbed her foot sinuously along his calf, relishing the intimate feel of the rough, coarse hair against her skin.

"Oh, *damn*—!"

"What!"

Realizing she'd spoken aloud, Edie hid her face in his shoulder, her words muffled and unintelligible.

"What's wrong, Edie? Come on, tell me." He smoothed her hair back gently.

"I, er, I just . . ."

"Just *what*?"

Her mumble was almost lost in the crook of his neck and when he finally understood what she'd said he stared down at her with a sharply incredulous look. Then he threw back his head and the hearty sound of his laughter suddenly filled the quiet room.

"Oh Edie, Edie," Daniel gasped at last, "you're marvelous." He hugged her, his shoulders still shaking with hilarity. "Who else but you, at a moment like this, would worry about whether or not she'd shaved her legs! God, you're incredible."

"Yeah," she mumbled, "incredible."

Oh Lord, how *tacky*.

She shook her head, mortified. "Sorry." She tried to free herself from his arms. She sure knew how to kill a mood: nobody could accuse *her* of sloppy sentimentality!

"What are you apologizing for? After all, Edie Calvin is truthful to the end, right?" Daniel hauled her back where he knew she belonged. His grin subsided to an indulgent smile as he gazed thoughtfully into the dark amber of her eyes.

"You know," he reflected, "it sounds unbelievable but I never knew before that sex could be *fun*. It always seemed so . . . oh, I don't know, so routine and . . . and clinical! Physically enjoyable, but—predictable." He nuzzled the top of her head, relishing the sweet, clean scent.

"I guess what I'm trying to say is, I wasn't ever totally *involved*." He chuckled dryly. "Of course, I seem to get 'totally involved' whenever I'm with you." Daniel hugged her and laughed like the young boy he'd never been. "It's . . . well, with you *nothing's* predictable! Ah, Edie, I feel so damn *good*—"

"Mm-hmm, you sure do." She was doing a little touching herself.

"—I *enjoy* myself, and you, and . . ." His eyes glowed warmly as he studied her face. "And I feel more alive and excited than I ever thought it was possible to be." He stared at her intently, then smiled easily again, with a new kind of lazy assurance, and whispered hoarsely in her ear. "And I have a feeling it's only going to get better."

Edie gazed up at him, her smile lighting the amber depths of her eyes. "Ahh, Daniel, you're a wonderful host. Is it time for dinner already?"

He laughed in delight. "Mmm," he nuzzled her neck as he rolled on top of her, hands and mouth busy. "I'm starving!"

He tasted her lips, nibbled at her throat, and lingered in the warm hollow where her pulse was quickening. His kiss flickered along the curve of her shoulder, nipping gently at the sensitive spot on the inside of her arm, and settled at last on the sensitive swell of her breasts. His tongue teased mercilessly until they rewarded him with renewed arousal, a reflection of the stirring in his own body.

This time their lovemaking assumed a gentler, easier pace. The urgent intensity was past and now they allowed themselves to know and savor all the sensations, the degrees of pleasure they could give each other. The air shimmered with soft moans, small sighs, and, sweetest of all, the tender laughter of lovers who truly enjoy the loving. Time was an alien thing in that room, and forgotten, as they learned each other, touched wellsprings of tenderness each had lost track of.

For Edie the beauty of these moments made her totally alive and aware, a feeling she hadn't known in too long. Daniel's was a sensitive, giving kind of love, though she knew he would never call it that. There wasn't a second when she could doubt how important her own pleasure was to him. She was almost giddy with the sudden intensity of her feelings.

Because she knew, with a knowledge far beyond rationality, that she loved Daniel Slayton as she would never, *could* never, love any other man. He might not return that love, but that wouldn't change anything. Perhaps he couldn't—perhaps he didn't know how. No matter. It was enough, for now, to share *her* love and these exquisite moments with *him*, allowing the fires of *her* passion to warm *him*.

Through her hands, her mouth, Edie felt Daniel's response: it echoed her own. Her sensitive fingers moved over his hot skin, as she had dreamed of doing from their first meeting. But now they knew, and understood, and *cared*, and it was so much better than she'd ever imagined it could be. His body spoke to her, telling her he shared the ecstasy with her.

Edie's fingers slid over the flat contours of his stomach and she felt the play of muscles quivering beneath taut skin. Down, past the crisp curls framing his sex, her shaking fingers stroked the hard, burning flesh. Daniel's reaction was instantaneous, a groan of overpowering pleasure that seemed torn from his very soul.

"My God, Edie . . . are you trying to kill me?"

She couldn't answer: her mouth was searing the flat plane of his belly with hot, biting kisses, her tongue teasing the sensitive flesh around his navel, flickering in and out with tantalizing precision.

Unable to withstand temptation another moment, Daniel swung over and raised himself above her, taking her hands and holding them outstretched on either side of her head. They stared at each other, entranced, as their bodies joined. An unnamed, unremembered glow of discovery blazed in his eyes and Daniel thrilled at the splendor that lit her face while he loved her.

Two very sleepy, very content, very happy people drifted into sleep, holding each other, protecting each other . . . needing each other.

"Mmmmm!" Edie blinked her half-open eyes and stretched leisurely, then lifted herself a bit to turn toward him, still within the circle of his arms.

Daniel came awake all at once, as he'd trained himself to do years ago when he was a resident on call at the hospital. He raised his head, placing a tender kiss on her eyelids, her temple. Then, pushing against the headboard, he hauled her back to him and they sat, gazing fondly at each other, foolish grins of smug self-satisfaction on their mouths.

With gentle fingers Edie reached up to brush from Daniel's forehead a stray lock of silver-flecked sable hair lying in a crescent just above his dark brows.

"I love you this way—"

"You look pretty good yourself," he said, leering at her nakedness.

"That too! No, I meant—oh, you're kind of rumpled, not so perfect." She twined the springy curl around her fingers.

"I wasn't perfect?"

She laughed and placed a big kiss in the middle of his chest. "Don't worry, we'll just keep doing it until you are." Suddenly Edie's eyes widened as a stray thought detached itself from her dreamy mind. She turned to stare at him, perplexed.

"Daniel, did you say your *wife* divorced *you*?"

He stiffened, nodded, a flash of distaste on his lean face.

"My God, the woman must be out of her tree!" Edie whispered with something akin to awe, sliding her arms more securely around him and nestling her head on his chest. She shook her head once, eyes closed, in amazed contemplation of such inconceivable stupidity. "How in the world did she let you go?" She clucked her tongue in disbelief. "I'm profoundly grateful, but she's obviously to be pitied; no matter how successful the woman is, she's not playing with a full deck."

Startled, Daniel smiled in delighted surprise at the artless candor of her spontaneous compliment. He settled deeper into the pillows, finding the most comfortable position, all the while stroking her shoulder, up and down her arm, retracing the same path in a rhythmic pattern, easing the persistent inner need to constantly prove to himself she was really there.

Incredible! He could not be the same Daniel Slayton who had always felt such nagging discomfort at even the least hint of intimacy.

"You have to understand, Edie, I've known Sandra ever since I can remember. Of course, we didn't have quite the same, uh, rapport that you and I seem to share." He smiled wryly and hugged her closer. "Our families were close and we lived in the same neighborhood—"

"Veddy, veddy exclusive!"

"—went to the same schools—"

"Veddy, veddy private!" She giggled when he pinched her.

"Anyway, no one, least of all us, was surprised by our marriage."

"Daniel," Edie asked, her voice low, suddenly hesitant, "did you . . . love her?"

"Love?" He grunted. "Ah, my sweet naive Edith Stephanie, I don't believe the thought ever occurred to either of us. It was a suitable match, that's all. We got along, we'd grown up with the same background, the same values—we thought. We just seemed like a good couple. The decision was perfectly logical."

"But," she protested, "logic has nothing to do with love!"

"Well, as it turned out, love had nothing to do with our marriage. Now, on the other hand, *logic*—!" A cynical smile stained the strong curve of his mouth for an instant. "Remember, Edie, a surgeon thinks in terms of pragmatic reality, methodical, precise, relying on verifiable phenomena. And, of course, Sandra is an extremely able lawyer. She's developed analytic logic to a fine art. She's a very precise, well-organized woman.

So our engagement and marriage were also very orderly, precise, and well organized.''

"What did they read at the ceremony—Robert's *Rules of Order*?" Edie muttered. "Geez, this is the damnedest conversation." But seeing the twisted humor in it, after all, she looked up at him blandly and winked. "I'll bet she never had to wonder if *her* legs were shaved."

"No," Daniel grinned, "not Sandra. Let's see, Monday and Thursday, she was in court; Friday we had dinner with friends; and on Saturday we caught up on errands, extra reading, she shaved her legs, and we had sex. I told you, we lived a very orderly life!"

"No picnics in the living room . . ."

"No pizza in my lap—in fact no pizza *or* picnics—so messy, you know."

"No vanilla ice cream in your shoes—"

"And no personal relationship with the dry cleaner, either!" Daniel kissed her with a sudden ferocity so new to him. "And no Edie! All those years without love in the afternoon: where were you when I needed you?"

She blinked up at him, the laughter suddenly fading. "Right here, Daniel." If she held him any tighter, she'd be behind him. "I'm right here, any time you want me."

She bit her lip at her thoughtless, impulsive remark. She'd better shut up, right now. How she felt, well, that was *her* problem.

"Daniel, why did you stay up here so late this year? Was it . . . the headaches?"

"Damn, you really know how to go for the bone, don't you?" He scowled and almost pulled away, but she held firm.

"Everyone knows the sweetest meat is next to the bone."

"There speaks a nosy, pushy busybody!"

"Absolutely right. Now—you were saying \ . . ?"

"Yeah, the headaches." With a resigned sigh, Daniel sank back into the pillows, brows raised, a wry twist to his lips. "Well, I've had 'em for a while, now. Maybe they should be considered a wedding present." He put his hands behind his head, gazing across the room unseeingly. "You know, when Sandra informed me she felt too 'restricted'—that was the word she used—and she didn't want to continue our marriage, I think I was surprised at how *unsurprised* I was. And how little I cared. Another profound truth I've discovered: a perfect wedding doesn't make a perfect marriage." He stopped for a moment, remembering, then shrugged.

"At any rate, there was a short, painless period of unwedded bliss and I buried myself deeper in my practice and my work at the hospital. Then they came back—much worse."

Edie frowned, a subtle dread beginning to gnaw inside her. "Have you consulted another doctor?" Her voice was tight and he stared at her, perplexed, then with dawning comprehension.

"Nothing serious," he murmured against the tangle of curls brushing her temple, "just tension and stress . . . the watchword of the decade! Of course, that was after I'd used up my supply of willpower and stubbornness, and a truckload of analgesics."

"*Analgesics?* My, my! Listen, Daniel, don't try to impress me with 'doctor talk'! You can just call them pain pills, like everyone else." Relieved, Edie giggled, then yelped when he tightened his grip on a curl and yanked.

"That'll teach you to have a little respect. No, forget it, you have too little respect already."

He hugged her, marveling anew at her quick concern, the very real fear he'd seen on her face. She did care! In his crumbling world it was a lifeline to cling to.

"A friend of mine happens to be an excellent neurologist. Sam and I ran a battery of tests and the unanimous diagnosis is the headaches are all in my head."

"Just what does *that* mean?"

"Physician, heal thyself." Daniel smiled reassuringly. "What it boils down to is I needed a good long rest."

And there it was.

"So, how long . . . before you go back?" Edie voiced her fear without conscious volition. It loomed so large she couldn't possibly avoid it.

For an instant Daniel's face tightened into a grim mask. He quickly smoothed it out into an easy, confident smile. "Well, who knows? Maybe never."

"Don't you know you should never say never?"

"But I've found certain . . . attractions . . . I really like up here. I might just stay on permanently."

"But, could you do that? What about your practice, your patients?"

"What about them? I have very able associates. There *are* other cardiac surgeons, as good and better than I. No, Edie, I'm not so egotistical as to think I'm indispensable. No one is, you know."

Her dubious expression revealed confusion and doubt. But she couldn't very well press the issue. And there was no need. He wouldn't stay up here, running away from his problems, not for long. He'd have to go back. That truth was never far from Edie's thoughts, as much as she tried to ignore it. But then, she'd never had any expectations of more than *here* and *now*. And, as he'd made very clear, *no one is indispensable*. She'd do well to remember that.

"Yes," Daniel stretched, a blandly innocent look on his face as he cautiously veered away from the disturbing thoughts their conversation had brought. "A nice rest, no stress, no strain, no aggravations." His mouth sketched an oblique smile as he glanced at her from the corner of his half-closed eyes. "Of course, I didn't count on you."

Edie just wrinkled her nose and stuck out her tongue.

"Oh, *that* was *good*! Befitting a witty, perceptive, mmfph . . ." His words were muffled beneath the pillow she suddenly flung at his head.

Amid the tangled bedding Daniel wrestled Edie to her back and was startled to feel her dissolve into an uncontrollable spasm of helpless giggles.

"Aha!" At that moment it was the most evil laugh she'd ever heard! "Ticklish, are we? Hmm, how about . . . here? And here, and . . . ?"

She fell back on the pillows, cheeks flushed, trying to catch her breath. "At last, we're even," he mumbled in her ear in a disgustingly smug tone of voice. "Even Dennis the Menace has an Achilles' heel."

"That's probably the only part of my body that isn't ticklish," she muttered.

"Now, isn't that interesting! Well, you can rest easy," he whispered into the side of her neck, "I'd never try to take advantage of your . . . weakness."

Edie looked at him, suspicion and disbelief on her face. "Me think you speak with forked tongue."

Daniel leered, wiggled his eyebrows, and leaned over her. "You wound me, madame, to . . . the . . . quick." He began to kiss her, systematically covering her face with a hundred soft, tiny kisses until he finally made his way to her breathless, parted lips. "And now—" He gently touched the corner of her mouth with the tip of his tongue and lazily traced the outline, licking a moist caress that started the electricity crackling through her all over again. Edie wasn't even aware she was breathing harder, shallower, and purring like a cat with a dish of pure cream.

"Forked tongue, hmm?" Daniel tasted the small hollow in the curve of her neck, then began to trace a dewy circle around her breasts, touching for a delicious moment the pebble-hard crest. She arched up to him, unable to stop trembling. Their only contact was the maddening tip of his tongue moving down her body, igniting glittering sparks across her skin.

"I'm just going to have to prove how wrong you are! I'll teach you to complain about my tongue."

"Oh Daniel," Edie sighed, "who's complaining?"

TEN

"Edith, you're late. And why is there a tree in your car?" Lillian closed the car door, careful to avoid damaging the leaves while she fended off the cozy embrace of an affectionate *Ficus Benjamina*.

"Oh, I picked it up just now at the mall for . . . somebody," Edie commented offhandedly, pulling out of the hospital parking lot. Wednesday was Lillian's volunteer day with the Hospital Guild and Edie picked her up after closing the drugstore.

Lillian would have had to be blind or stupid, or both—and she was neither—not to know that Daniel Slayton was certainly "somebody." Yes indeed.

"Does Daniel like plants?" she asked ingenuously.

"I hope so. It's a surpr—" Edie turned to stare at her mother, noting the guileless twinkle in the older woman's eyes.

Edie laughed. "That obvious, huh?"

"Like Rudolph's nose, sweetie."

"You're too damned—darned—smart for my own good," Edie sighed in exasperation. "I swear, I can't seem to get through fifteen minutes without thinking about him, trying to make him happy."

142

Something in her voice caught Lillian's ear, more than the words.

"Now, why do you feel you have to *make* him happy? Is something wrong, honey?"

"Oh Lord, Mom, the man's so . . . so . . . And his *house*, it's really . . . He needs to . . . I mean, he never even saw 'The Blob' . . . and they didn't laugh . . ." She stopped for a quick breath.

"Er, yes, of course."

By now they'd pulled up the snow-rimmed driveway of their house. Edie's words stumbled to a halt and she felt a painful stab of disloyalty. She'd almost revealed a private part of Daniel, things he'd trusted her with. It would have been a betrayal, inexcusable even in the incoherent babblings of a moonstruck teenager, which she was coming to resemble in an alarming fashion. Especially since "Super Sunday."

Lillian, sensing her discomfort, asked no more: she understood enough. They dragged the plants into the back hall and as they removed their boots she studied her daughter thoughtfully.

"Honey, I think you're probably headed in the right direction. If he were hungry, you'd give him food, wouldn't you? Well, sometimes other things are just as important. Whatever he needs, if you care enough . . ."

Setting the table while Lillian took a soup pot from the refrigerator and turned on the stove, Edie gave voice to the doubts and questions churning in her mind.

"Tell you the truth, I'm in a muddle. How do I know I'm right? I keep remembering Mark. I was positively obsessed, and look what a mistake *that* was! My God, if you only knew—"

"Sweetheart," Lillian broke in quietly, "I knew. Because I know you. I could read between the lines, even when you didn't write the lines. Oh, not the details, though I can guess." She stopped stirring soup for a moment, her mouth twisted grimly, and Edie stared, astonished at her mother's insight. "But you're older now, and wiser I think, and you have to ask yourself if your feelings for Daniel are anything at all like those you felt for . . . for him." She couldn't bring herself, even now, to speak the name of the man who had so callously hurt her child.

Edie studied her mother, astounded anew by the depth of the woman's understanding. Those unhappy years with Mark: she'd known! All along, Lillian had known . . . something. And yet she'd never pried, never interfered—and most blessedly, had never once, by the least inflection of voice or glance, even implied an I-told-you-so.

"Oh Mom, that son of a bitch didn't deserve a mother-in-law like you!" Edie walked around the table and hugged her, holding back the quick tears of love and appreciation.

"Now, you see, I don't have to worry about you. Your judgment and your instincts are very sound." Teary-eyed, Lillian smiled with confidence at the younger edition of herself. "As your father used to say, God rest his soul, 'Your head is screwed on right.' "

She began to ladle soup and meat into the bowls. "And you know, I think you've already made your decision." Lillian smiled a small secret smile, pleased at the thought, pleased with the woman her daughter had become. *We've raised a lovely girl, Jacob. You'd be so proud.*

A very thoughtful Edie was suddenly, consciously aware of the person her mother was. Lillian, the unending source of warmth and love, approval and concern Edie had taken for granted all her life. And in the bright clarity of her insight she ached for what she knew Daniel had missed.

They say you don't miss what you've never had.

What a damnable lie.

*   *   *

"Hi! Can Danny please come out and play?"

Dangling from Edie's extended index finger was a worn pair of ice skates, the black leather cracked with age but the blades polished and gleaming. Her father had gotten many a winter's use out of them and she hoped they'd fit Daniel. She'd take odds he hadn't any of his own.

"Wh—? Edie! What are you doing here?"

The blank surprise on his face gave way to a wide grin of delight. He reached for her, dragging her inside and into his arms. "You're not a mirage!" His kiss was thorough, exploring again a well-known and increasingly desirable terrain. He hadn't begun to understand the depths of his hunger for her, not until he saw her standing there, her tousled hair wreathed in the golden shimmer of bright November sunshine.

Her mouth opened to him at his first touch. Nothing hesitant, nothing tentative. Nothing but joy, the giving and taking of pleasure. Unnoticed, the skates slid through her suddenly nerveless fingers and thudded to the floor. An aura of infinite happiness was almost palpable in the quiet house by the frozen lake. For the moment the only intrusion was the lush melody of a Beethoven sonata filtering into the hall from the living room.

"It's your . . . Sunday to . . . work, isn't it?" he murmured, covering her face with a string of fervent kisses. It was an exuberant display so alien to the man he'd always been that he suddenly had to laugh at himself.

"What's so funny, hmm?" Edie leaned back in his arms, head cocked inquisitively to one side. The irrepressible grin she couldn't hold back lit her face. Her pulse beat furiously and her throat was so tight she could hardly force out the words. God, he was so beautiful!

"Me! Us!" Daniel laughed. "What am I doing in the middle of the afternoon, standing here hugging and kissing a woman who's got me so crazy I can't keep my hands off her?" He shook his head, in awe at the changes he saw in himself. Beneath the laughter coiled a faint stir of unease, and perhaps fear, fear of his own weakness for her, fear of something unknown. Resolutely he ignored it.

"Edith Stephanie Calvin, what the hell have you done to me? And whatever it is, don't stop." He pulled her closer and her answer was trapped in the heat of his mouth. He kissed her deeply, thoroughly, and she forgot everything else.

"Hey," he asked hoarsely, "you didn't answer my question. What are you doing here?" His raspy breath touched her ear and a shudder skittered across her shoulder blades.

"I can't talk and kiss at the same time. Which will it be?" Edie asked hopefully.

"Talk first, kiss later," he chuckled. "I'm a practical man. If we start kissing, we may never talk."

"Spoilsport." She made a face. "Anyway, it's a holiday! Mr. Mac's back home, so I've got the day off, if I want."

Ah, she wanted. Edie was very much afraid, the way she felt right now, she wanted too much. Because Daniel might never be willing, or even able, to give that much.

"And I have some news, actually something I want to ask you about." She took a deep breath. "Mr. Mac wants me to buy the drugstore."

"What?" Daniel took her hands in his. "That's wonderful! What happened?"

"He had such a great time on his vacation he decided it was time he and Mrs. M. began to really enjoy themselves. So he asked if I'd be interested." She frowned, uneasy at the sudden appearance of commitment, then shrugged. "I said I'd think about it and let him know. It's an awfully big decision and I don't want to rush it." Her face brightened suddenly. "Anyway, we can talk about it later. Right now we'd better hurry, while the sun's still out. Oh, I almost forgot—do you skate?"

"Yeah, I wondered when you'd get around to that." Daniel looked doubtful, confronted by the imminent reality of her plans for the day. "I used to, a little, but not for years."

Edie grinned and pushed him toward the closet. "C'mon, Daniel, it'll be lots of fun. We used to do it all the time when I was a kid. And the ice looks great today." A subzero cold wave, the "Siberian Express" down from Canada, had solidified the whole northern half of the state over the last week. If no one else was cheered, ice skaters, hockey players, and heating pad salesmen were in their glory. Right now, Daniel was not.

"Yeah, fun." He sounded definitely unconvinced. "Uh, maybe there's an old horror movie on TV," he hinted, to no avail. Daniel cocked a dubious glance at the glowing fireplace, then at her determined face, and it was no contest. Oh well, with Edie it probably *would* be fun. It wouldn't be boring.

"Daniel, you're not chicken, are you?" she teased.

"My dearest Edie, before I met you it was my religion. I was a devout coward." They grinned at each other while he pulled on his jacket and a pair of fur-lined gloves. "And since our first meeting I'm more convinced than ever that I was right." He picked up the skates where she'd dropped them and ushered her out the door.

"Oh wait, Daniel—they'll die in the car."

"What? Who?" Startled, he peered in the window. "There's a tree growing in your car."

"My mother beat you to it," she mumbled, dragging

it and a smaller plant out onto the drive. "It . . . it's a present."

"For me?" He stared in blank surprise.

"Oh, look," she said, suddenly shy and unsure in the face of his continued silence, "I just happened to see them at the mall and . . . well, if you don't care for them, I'll take them back. Honestly, it's no big deal." She started to retrieve them.

A strangely sweet smile touched Daniel's face, erasing the shock. "It's a very big deal." He forestalled her and gently cupped her reddened cheek with one leather-gloved hand. "And I do care . . . I care very much."

Edie was quite sure it was only the severe cold that prevented her from melting into a puddle in the middle of his driveway. Oh wonderful! The perfect example of twentieth-century *Femalus Liberatus*!

Together they dragged the things she'd brought into the house, then continued to the ice-bound lake. With fingers already almost numb from cold they laced on their skates and took the first tentative steps away from shore.

Edie waved a mittened hand toward a far-distant corner of the lake where a group of small, colorfully dressed figures chased each other in circles around a small area near the opposite shore. "Oh look, way over there, see? The kids still use the same spot for skating." Her laughter was infectious. "What a perfectly marvelous day!"

"Thank God they're over there. The lack of witnesses is my only consolation."

Edie looked down to see Daniel slowly rising to his shaky feet, brushing off his snow-covered behind. She hadn't even seen him go down. But she heard him clearly enough.

"Tottering around like a drunken clown . . . cold enough to freeze the . . . ears off a brass monkey. If

God meant for people to navigate on ice, we'd have been born with scotch and soda in our veins.''

"Now, now, Daniel," Edie choked back a laugh, trying to placate him. "You're doing fine."

He looked up at her quizzically as his feet flew out from under him and he took abrupt repossession of his seat on the frozen surface. He made no move to get up, just sat there leaning back on his hands. "You sure this is fun? Because if I were having any more fun I'd be in traction."

"Oh, come on, people do this all over the world. They can't all be crazy—"

"Why not?"

"It *is* fun, you'll see. Come on now, we'll try again."

"What's this 'we' business? *You're* still standing upright and *I'm* horizontal! Say," he tilted his head and squinted up at her, "is this what they mean by déjà vu or have we done this before? I don't think I enjoyed it all that much the first time."

"Dammit, Daniel, you get up this minute! You're going to have fun whether you like it or not!"

They glared at each other, cloud wisps of breath dissipating in the chill air, and the absurdity of her words sunk in. Their laughter pealed sharply in the bright, brittle sunshine.

At last he shook his head and sighed in resignation. "Okay, okay, I seem to have an unsuspected streak of masochism fighting for expression. If at first you don't succeed . . . you ought to quit," Daniel declaimed mockingly, heaving his body upright and swearing he would definitely have a good time, right up until the ambulance took him away.

"Okay, you turkey," Edie shook a fist at him, "this time you're gonna do it!" And, he thanked heaven, finally she was right. Long-forgotten memories came back and Daniel did just fine. For the rest of the afternoon their enjoyment equaled, and maybe surpassed, that of the children across the lake.

Later, weary feet propped on the no-longer inviolate table, they thawed their frozen bones before the fire, drinking mugs of hot chocolate to the accompaniment of the rest of the Beethoven.

"Damn good thing I finally got the hang of it; I have a fond desire to reach old age with all my original parts."

Edie silently agreed. They were wonderful parts.

"Yep," he continued smugly, "I really was pretty good out there, you know? Next time maybe we can try skating backwards."

Edie, snug in the shelter of Daniel's arm, nodded sleepily. She noted with approval that "next time" and smiled, especially content as she glanced around the room at their jackets dangling carelessly defiant on the crystal clothes tree. That prized specimen had seen better days.

Or perhaps not. Could any day be better than this? She admired the bright accent of glossy plants and the splash of colorful pillows tossed next to the hearth. The room had metamorphosed from a study in cold perfection into a comfortable, happy oasis of warmth and welcome.

"Do you feel like a miracle worker?" As if he were reading her mind, Daniel's tender glance deepened and he placed a soft kiss on top of Edie's bent head. "You are, you know. Really," he stopped her question, "you have definitely made miracles here. And in the house, too," he chuckled, hugging her so close they almost took a bath in hot chocolate. He settled deeper into the couch and groaned, shifting weight off his much-punished rear.

"Aagh! That's what I get for worshipping Our Lady of the Perpetual Bruises."

"Oh, you ingrate. You know you had a great time!"

"Ah yes, every aching, throbbing bone and muscle in my body thanks you from the bottom of its black and blue. I think I'll spend the next few days vertical. Anything else would be too damn painful," he moaned.

With a grin Edie slowly rose, took his mug, and placed it with hers amid the newspapers and books on the table. She turned and pulled a pitifully groaning Daniel to his stockinged feet and slid her arms around to the back of his waist. Her hands worked their way down underneath his belt, and she began to slowly stroke and massage the taut muscles. Rising on tiptoes Edie gently nibbled on Daniel's earlobe and, eyes sparkling, whispered suggestively in his ear. A smile of anticipation blossomed on his face; other parts of his body began to blossom, too.

"Of course, there are still one or two things I can do horizontally."

"And I promise you won't feel any pain at all."

She was absolutely right.

The next weekend Edie gleefully dragged Daniel to the nearby town of Cadillac for the glories of a Boris Karloff festival. They passed the evening elbow deep in popcorn and Milk Duds while a late-blooming Daniel learned the mysteries of Egyptian mummies, dirty bandages, tanna leaves, and monsters with bolts in their necks and seams in their foreheads.

"Pass the Milk Duds, please," she whispered.

"There aren't any more."

"Whaaat—you *finished* them *all*?" Incredulous, her voice rose to a loud squeal.

"Quiet!" The stern voice shushed them out of the darkness of the theater.

"Shh . . . I'll get you more," Daniel promised.

"The candy counter is closed!" she hissed.

"My, my, I never thought you'd turn vicious. Anyway, I was only trying to help you stick to your diet,'' he lied virtuously.

"What are you, the world's oldest Boy Scout, or a Richard Simmons groupie?"

"Hey, lady, I'll give you *my* candy! Just let us hear the end of the movie! Please!"

"It's going to end the same way it always does," Edie muttered. "He won't get the girl." Miserable grouch!

A red-faced Daniel scrunched down in silence, trying to blend in with the upholstery. He hurried her out when the credits were barely finished, before the lights went up.

"I know how Dr. Frankenstein felt when the mob got ugly and came after him," he scolded, pulling her through the parking lot.

"Very funny. Hmph! Some people get so testy over the least little thing."

"Ha! You dare to talk? Milk Duds!"

"Oh? Are they too plebeian for you? I suppose if it were caviar—!"

They reached the car and he pulled her into the shadows. "Edie, did anyone ever tell you you talk too much?"

"Yes, frequently, but—"

Daniel proceeded to smother the rest of her remarks with the most effective method he could think of. It took at least two seconds for her arms to wind around his neck and her body to cling to his.

"Mmm, I've got the candy man, forget the Milk Duds."

There were long, lazy evenings; sometimes they played chess, at which Edie's strategy was not terribly effective.

"Daniel, are you sure you're not using more than thirty-two pieces?"

Other nights they played Casino with Lillian, Daniel unwarned by a vengeful Edie of her mother's tendency to go for the jugular at the card table. He was a gracious loser.

And they talked. There was so much to learn, and in both the flickering apprehension that maybe, just maybe, there would be too little time. The future was studiously avoided. Like a dry sponge, Daniel absorbed the atmosphere of a happy house, and stored up memories. And he basked in the affection, and chocolate chip cookies, showered on him by a beaming Lillian.

"You're shameless," Edie scolded, not really meaning it. She knew how little of it he'd had in his life. "She adores you and you just let her wait on you hand and foot."

"But she seems to enjoy it," he protested innocently. "I only do it to make her happy."

"Daniel, this is Sarah Detwiler. She and Stan own this place. We all went to school together, sometime after the Civil War."

"Hi, Sarah." He smiled down at her and the swelling evidence of an imminent new Detwiler. "Nice to meet . . . all of you."

"Pretty soon—I hope—you'll be seeing a lot *less* of me." She ducked her head and stage whispered in the general vicinity of the eight and a half month bulge. "Hurry up, will ya, kid? We're all gettin' kind of antsy out here!"

Their laughter was suddenly interrupted by a small blond tornado catapulting from the back room and around the counter.

"Mom, *Mom*, he's staring at me!"

The complaint was rife with six-year-old outrage, followed by consternation when he saw he had an unexpected audience. The cause of his older brother's indignation followed close on the complainant's heels, as quickly as his chubby, almost four-year-old legs could carry him. He stared up at them, a misunderstood angel with two clear blue, blatantly innocent eyes, a barely perceptible wobble beginning on his pouty lower lip.

"Hi, Edie." His face brightened as he spotted a potential ally. Edie winked, smiling broadly at the pint-sized con artist.

"Kevin, he wasn't staring at you," Sarah consoled her older son. "Brian, stop staring at your brother."

She shrugged, a wry smile in the face of the semi-confusion registered on all faces present. "The prime rule of motherhood: if it's said with authority, it doesn't have to make sense."

At that moment one tear rolled dramatically down the chubby pink cheek of the small accused.

"Mobby," he sniffed, "Kevin said I'm too dumb to go to school." Two more tears appeared. "Tell 'im I'm not, either!"

"Are, too!"

"Are not!"

"Are!"

"Not!"

"STOP!" The harried bellow erupting from the diminutive, soft-spoken Sarah brought all heads snapping around in shock, and absolutely stopped the two miniature blond combatants in their tracks, their mouths agape.

"Boy, I can't wait to get them home. As soon as Stan gets back from the bank, I'm gone!" Then, contrite at her impatience, knowing it stemmed more from her own physical discomfort than their boisterous behavior, she moved quickly. "Here, you guys, how about some cookies until din—"

As Sarah bent down for the box, she gasped, face contorted with an anguished spasm of pain. She gripped the shelf for a moment, then straightened as it passed.

"Sarah! What is it?" But Edie already knew.

"Edie, call Doctor Dressler, the number's in— aaagh!" She doubled over again, her body writhing as if jabbed by a red-hot poker, beads of perspiration standing out on her forehead and upper lip.

Daniel quickly reached for Sarah's hand, letting her squeeze his fingers bloodless as he helped her down to the floor. "Edie," he said firmly, "hurry, get me a carton of disposable diapers, or even some newspapers, and spread them out here."

Sarah bit her lips trying unsuccessfully to stifle the groan that drew the attention of two wide-open pairs of worried blue eyes, watching in awe from where the small boys huddled together. Curiosity overrode fear and worry as they studied the tall man holding their mother's hand where she knelt on the floor.

"Steady now, Sarah. Take small panting breaths." Without thought Daniel took charge, assuming an air of command he wore quietly and naturally, assessing what had to be done and moving calmly to do it with authority and quick competence. Edie watched him with quiet pride while she quickly prepared, at his direction, an impromptu labor room on the grocery floor.

"Sure . . . glad we keep . . . this place . . . so clean," Sarah gasped with a wan, frightened smile as she clutched Daniel's hand.

"I'm s-s-sorry, Mommy." Kevin's contrite whisper was guilt stricken.

"Hey, Kevin," Daniel turned quickly to the older boy, alert to the forlorn look on his frightened little face. "There's nothing to be sorry about. Everything's fine." His voice was cheerful, reassuring, easing the awful sense of self-condemnation in which the child was already caught. Daniel knew, and he saw on Edie's face the same knowledge, the terrible legacy this trauma could leave in a young, innocent mind, no matter how guiltless the reality.

"Your baby brother decided he wants to meet you two guys now." Daniel grinned at them. "Can't say I blame him for not wanting to wait. He's gonna be pretty lucky to have a pair of brothers like you two!"

A muffled groan from Sarah held his attention for a moment, then he turned back to Kevin, Brian hanging back uncertainly behind the now-welcome security of his big brother.

"Look, fellas, I'm a doctor, so I'm going to help your mom and the baby until we get them to the hospital. Tell you the truth, I could use some help." Daniel lowered his voice to a conspiratorial whisper. "Kevin, why don't you take Edie in back and show her where the telephone is?" He smiled and signaled Edie with his eyes to get the boys away from the scene of the impending birth, all the while massaging the distended bulk of Sarah's contracting belly.

"And Brian," he added to the white-faced four-year-old, "why don't you hold Edie's hand so she won't be scared, okay?" He winked at the towhead, an immediate man-to-man understanding established.

The two boys eagerly joined in his plan, at once absolved of guilt and given the importance his whispered charge had conferred on them. "C'mon, Edie," her very protective companions pulled her hand, "you don't have to worry. Daddy will be back soon."

"Okay, guys." Edie let them steer her into the back room. "Let's see what's on TV while I call Doctor Dressler, okay?" She turned on the small set Sarah kept back there, turning the volume louder than usual, her smile hiding her worry. Sarah had told her sons about the new baby, but she certainly hadn't planned on their participation. Edie glanced absently at the flickering screen while the phone rang. Thank God for Wally and the Beaver! She quickly told the doctor's receptionist what was happening, then settled down on the floor between her young guardians as they awaited the arrival of the ambulance and the doctor.

"All right, fellas, did that rotten Eddie Haskell get the Beaver in trouble again?"

As it happened, the newest addition to the Detwiler clan, like time and tide, waited for no man, neither doctor nor daddy. With sudden squalling impatience she chose to make her debut on her own terms, and it was Daniel's steady hands that welcomed Elizabeth Danielle Detwiler to her new family.

ELEVEN

The attendants carefully placed Sarah on the stretcher and packed away their instruments. Pale and exhausted, she looked up at Edie and clutched her hand.

"Talk about being in the right place at the right time! Thank God your timing's so good." She smiled weakly and turned her head. "And it's certainly been memorable meeting *you*, Daniel. I'll bet that's one introduction you'll never forget, either." With a proud smile she looked down at the tiny bundle of humanity squirming restlessly in the blanket on her mother's recently flattened abdomen. "But she is sweet, isn't she?"

"She's great!" Daniel marveled, beaming. Looking at the fragile bit of life he'd just held in his hands, he felt inordinately pleased with himself. The unique, singularly beautiful miracle of birth was a marvel he hadn't witnessed for many years, not since his internship. He'd forgotten how awesome and satisfying it was.

"And I don't look like Frosty the Snowman anymore," Sarah quipped as her eyes drooped, fatigue finally taking its toll.

A stunned but grateful Stan Detwiler took Daniel

aside while Edie tucked the blanket firmly around his wife. "Doctor Dressler told me how close it was. I don't think I'll ever be able to thank you enough for . . ." He choked, eyes wet with tears of gratitude. He pumped Daniel's hand, hurriedly hugged Edie, and stumbled into the ambulance with his wife and daughter.

"Well, young man," Dr. Dressler grinned in approval as he prepared to leave, "you're even more close-mouthed than my wife when she's mad at me. All these years you've been coming up here and no one knowing you're a surgeon." He shook his bald head. "Pretty smart, at that, now that I think of it. Only way to get any peace and quiet without having to listen to symptoms all day! Can't figure how you managed to fool the local snoops, though. Doesn't happen often, let me tell you." Edie laughed in agreement and Daniel offered a diffident shrug.

"Anyway, glad you were on the scene." The doctor laid a large hand on Daniel's arm. "That little girl's starting off with some pretty good luck. With the cord twisted around her neck that way—" He stopped, stared down at the floor for a moment, lost in thought, then shook his head, face grim. "Well . . . you've got good hands. We can all thank God you were here!" He turned and reached for his coat. "Told Sarah she was close, but I never thought it'd be *this* close."

The gruff-voiced doctor struggled into his coat and jammed his hat on his head. "And as for you, young lady, when am I going to have *you* for a patient, hmmm? What are you waiting for?" Before a red-faced Edie could sputter out an answer he swung back to Daniel, who was enjoying immensely this sudden turn in the conversation. "Well, better get going. But I'll tell you, son, you ever want to take up permanent residence and give general practice a try, look me up any time—" Then he walked out of the store to his car and followed his patients to the hospital, unaware of the sudden pallor of Daniel's face and a corresponding gleam of comprehension in Edie's eyes.

Daniel, deliberately ignoring the doctor's last words, slumped down on the comfortable old couch and shifted his leg, careful not to disturb Lorraine. "Well, I've got to hand it to you, Miss Calvin. There's nothing conventional about you, is there? I mean, when you plan a day—wow! What could you possibly do to top this one?" Stretching his legs luxuriously toward the fire, hands folded behind his head, Daniel regarded her fondly through half-lowered lids, a lazy, contented smile on his mouth.

After explaining—and they weren't sure how successfully—that girls "really weren't so bad," they'd stuffed Kevin and Brian with burgers, fries, and ice cream to their hearts' and stomachs' content and deposited them with their grandparents. It had been a revelation to Edie, those two small blond boys and the large dark-haired man, forming that instant affectionate alliance. How marvelous he was with them! He'd have made a wonderful father, she thought wistfully, irrationally angry at the unknown Sandra for cheating him of the chance.

Now she sat down carefully at the other end of the couch and avoided looking at him. "You know, Daniel, it sounds strange but today I *saw* you, *all* of you, for the first time. It was—" She stopped, not sure how to explain, not sure she understood it herself. "You were . . . impressive." He was wonderful. "The way you took charge, talking Sarah through it that way, keeping her—all of us—so calm." She recalled vividly her own shaken state before Daniel's steady, controlled precision smoothed the jagged edge of anxiety. In the face of her momentary paralysis he had, with a few concise words and deft actions, reduced the numb helplessness that had bubbled so near the surface.

"If it hadn't been for you, that baby wouldn't have made it, would she? And instead of a horrible guilt trip those two little boys shared a beautiful experience. And . . . you did it."

For a few moments she'd stood in the doorway, behind her the two small faces turned to the flickering TV screen, and watched Daniel bring that small life safely on its first journey, his big hands so gentle, so sure— and she had known. What a very fine surgeon he must be, she'd thought, and how fortunate those patients who came under his care, their lives in the balance and his skilled hands the deciding factor. It was a memory she would treasure always. And it was a moment that crystallized quite clearly what she sensed, and feared, was inevitable. "It's been quite a while, hasn't it, since you played doctor?"

He raised his brows and grinned slyly, reaching for her. "There are much better ways to play doctor." But her expression stopped him and he suddenly became aware of the undercurrent in Edie's voice. "Why should that bother you?" Wary now, and alert, Daniel sat up straighter. "And you are bothered, aren't you? Is it because you were so forcibly reminded that I *am* a doctor?" he demanded. "Damn, don't tell me we're back to that again. I thought we were long past that garbage!"

Edie raised her head, startled, and stared at him. "No! Oh *no*, Daniel, it's not that, *never* that. Believe me, no one knows better than I there's not the slightest resemblance between you and Mark, except the M.D. after your names. No matter *what* he did he could *never* be the man you are!" Her voice cracked and she ducked her head, unable to look at him. "I was so very proud of you today, and so grateful. My God, what would

Sarah have done without you?" *What would I do without you?* "I guess that's the trouble."

"What the hell are you talking about? *What's* the trouble? Look, stop talking in riddles." Annoyed and worried, and not even sure just why, Daniel rose swiftly and pulled her close. "Is this trouble?" he whispered hoarsely, kissing her with a kind of repressed fury born of desperation and fear. He moved his mouth over hers, searching, tasting every sweet secret, stroking her skin with his lips, his tongue, in a relentless caress.

Her body, her mind, were consumed with the exquisite excitement he could summon so easily with his touch. Hadn't it always been like this?

It wasn't—couldn't be—enough. She backed away.

"I think you must be a very fine surgeon. Much too good to hide up here forever. It would be such a terrible waste. And *that's* trouble, isn't it? The work you do is too important, too many people depend on your skill. And you love doing it, don't you?" She jammed her hands deep into her jeans pockets and turned away to stare fixedly out the window into the darkness. "Look, Daniel, I don't know what happened back there, what you're running away from, but whatever it is, you can't turn your back and pretend it doesn't exist. Sooner or later you'll have to face it."

Well, she'd finally said it. Unwanted. Unpleasant. But still the truth, the truth she could no longer avoid. Deflated now, and unsure, she leaned wearily against the window, staring down blindly at the worn carpet, memorizing again the intricacies of its faded floral pattern. The room was absolutely silent.

"Who the *hell* do you think you are? *What gives you the right to decide what I need, what I have to do?* And just who appointed you to be my conscience, anyway?"

Her head whipped around in shock at the cold rage in his words, the glacial frost in the stare he aimed with the effect of a deadly weapon. It was not the reaction she'd anticipated.

"But this—it isn't a question of rights, it's what's right for *you*!" His affronted expression was suddenly too much. "Oh, come off it, Daniel, you carry the past around your neck like some damned *albatross*. Face it and get rid of it once and for all."

Like some fearsome monolith Daniel towered menacingly above her, but despite the inner quaking she didn't give an inch. He inhaled a huge breath and, fists clenched stiffly at his sides, stalked to the fireplace. He deliberately forced his fingers open and, bracing his arms against the mantel, stared into the flames, willing himself to smother emotion. At last he turned back, the fire in his eyes banked behind a wall of gray ice.

"Of course, you're right. I turned my back on that other part of my life and came here to hide." His mouth twisted in a bitter sneer. "It wasn't much of a choice, because it really wasn't much of a life." He took a breath. "Damn you! Can't you understand, if I ran it was because I *had* no choice!"

He rubbed his head, a gesture in deference to an old habit, a gesture he hadn't made, or needed to make, for weeks. When he spoke again, his tone was clinical, colorless. "I'm a surgeon, Edie, a cardiovascular surgeon. That means when I walk into that O.R. I *literally* hold my patient's life pulsing in my hands. They have to be steady hands, dependable hands." He stared down at them as if he didn't know what they were. "And when I become more dangerous than the disease, I'd damn well better turn and run." His dead voice stunned her more than his words.

He flicked a cold glance at her. "I've never found much satisfaction in my family and personal relationships, and I was obviously a less than outstanding husband. But when it came to professional performance, by God, *I was the best*. And I proved it with a vengeance! All I had left was work, and if it was going to be my life, then nothing . . . *nothing* . . . would come between it and me." His jaw was rigid. "Nothing except the pain."

His stare was cold, implacable, and Edie couldn't look away. "You want to know why I choose to stay up here, to 'hide' up here? *I almost killed a child, that's why!*" He held his thumb and forefinger together with a hair's breadth between. "Seven years old, innocent, his whole life ahead of him, and that's how close I came to severing his aorta and ending it all for him. And it wasn't because of any unavoidable or unexpected surgical complication. No, I was just too stubborn, too proud, too damned *indispensable* to postpone surgery or call in another man."

Daniel jammed shaking hands into his pockets to hide, instinctively, the evidence of his shattered control. "Of course, taking medication before surgery was out of the question. But I couldn't ignore it anymore, either."

He felt afresh the blinding agony of that terrible morning. "I stood there, in that operating room, my hands were shaking and I literally *could not see*. I almost . . . I might have . . ." He swallowed with visible effort. "Thank God I had an extremely able assistant with the guts to push me aside before I—"

He repressed a shudder at the horrifying memory. "That was seven months ago. I haven't set foot in a hospital since." Daniel shook his head in weariness and slumped into a chair, rubbing a hand over his ashen face.

"I will never—I *can't* ever—take that chance again."

The ticking of a clock somewhere in the empty house and the sudden crack of a shifting log in the fireplace were the only counterpoint to his words. A faint shadow of dark beard accentuated the flat planes of his cheeks, the slight hollow beneath.

But Edie saw more than that. She saw the rock-steady dependability behind his hard look and distant attitude. No matter what he thought of himself, there was a granite core of strength and honesty to back up his training and judgment and those excellent hands of his. And, perhaps more important than anything else, there was a gentle, tender man, a man who could feel joy and desire, who could understand the workings of a child's mind and feelings, and take the time to be careful of them, as he had done today. A man like that was too valuable, too precious to abandon. Her instinct told her he wouldn't need someone else to keep him from endangering a patient, to push him aside: he'd do it himself. His innate integrity would have allowed nothing less. Why wasn't he aware of that, too? Had no one ever shown him, told him? There might be more she had to learn about him, but there was a lot he had to learn about himself.

"How frequent were the headaches?" Her question was asked with surprising detachment.

He shrugged. "Almost constant."

"When was the last one?" For a few seconds she thought he hadn't heard.

"It's been . . . weeks now. I suppose that day you filled my prescription." He lifted his head slowly. "I haven't used it since that night."

"So, it's a draw."

He looked at her, uncomprehending.

"You almost lost a child. And today you saved one."

Their gazes locked and Daniel stared as if he'd never seen her before. He shook his head once, frowning, and began to walk around the familiar room, as if searching for answers, touching the back of the couch, a lamp, the mantel—orienting himself to a world he was suddenly unsure of.

It was that precise moment that a loud burp from

beneath the table intruded unexpectedly. It was an extremely effective break in the almost unbearable tension, and both Edie and Daniel were grateful for it. Sensing their attention, Lorraine let her perpetually gloomy face beam up at them foolishly with what might conceivably pass for a basset hound grin.

"I think maybe she's telling me it's getting late. I guess I'd better be going." Daniel rose. "It's been a rough day all around and I've got some thinking to do." Edie's smile was shaky and she reached out to take his hand.

"At least now it's out in the open you can face it. A problem can't be solved unless you admit there's a problem. You have to just let it happen, Daniel. Things will sort themselves out."

"Sounds like something your mother would say," he observed dryly.

"You learn fast." Edie smiled. "She'll be upset she missed you. She looks forward to your visits." She tipped her head, studying him. "Funny, here we are, in the middle of the twentieth century—you know, women's lib, civil rights, assertiveness training—and you've managed to install yourself in the middle of your own private harem. My mother would lie down and let you wipe your shoes on her, and *thank* you for the privilege. That rotten dog actually quivers with excitement the minute you walk in the door. Hell, she'd probably even share her beer and ice cream with you!" She frowned in mock disgust.

"And you?" Daniel asked intently. Edie was leaning against the front door and he stood in front of her, one hand braced on the door frame beside her head. She was trapped, and she wouldn't have minded being trapped forever.

"Me?" Edie's smile couldn't hide the depth of her feelings. "I'd fight my mother, the dog, a tribe of Amazons just to be first in line." The smile faded as her eyes burned him with the intensity of her feelings. "How come you don't know that?"

They stared at each other in the dim light of the hall. Daniel's throat was so dry he couldn't swallow. And he couldn't speak—still could not speak the words she longed to hear, the words strangling in his throat. Too much history, too many thoughts and decisions lay between them before he could look to the future. He was fighting to overcome a life's worth of repression—and the last lingering tendrils of distrust.

Instead, he pulled her close, trying to show with his hard, almost brutal kiss what he couldn't say any other way. He needed to bury the oppressive past, was afraid of investing hope in an ambiguous future; and so he was trapped, in an inconclusive and evanescent present. With an abrupt movement he thrust her away and turned to the door. "I've got to get out of here," he said with barely leashed violence. And then he was gone.

Edie was standing where he'd left her, unshed tears clinging to her lashes, when his car turned the corner and disappeared.

TWELVE

"Mom? That you?" Edie rose wearily from the couch when she heard Lillian fumbling with the door. She'd hoped to have a couple of hours to recover from the scene with Daniel before she had to face her mother. "What are you doing home this early?" She bent to kiss the cheek that was strangely cold, damp. "I thought you—Mother, what's the matter? You look—my God, *what's wrong!*"

Wordless, the older woman fell into the chair beside the front door, still wearing her coat, scarf slipping carelessly off her head, gloves dropping unnoticed beside her feet. The unhealthy gray pallor of Lillian's face and the clammy film of perspiration that shone on her skin told Edie something was dreadfully wrong.

"I—I don't know what . . ." Lillian gasped, struggling painfully for each breath. Suddenly she clutched her chest and doubled over, gasping. "I think I . . . Edie, help—" She slid from the chair in a crumpled heap.

"Oh, God, oh no! No, please God, please, please . . ." Petrified, Edie felt for the weak pulse, thready and uneven, then dashed to the phone, still muttering frantic, incoherent prayers. Panic numbed her fingers as they fumbled at the dial until finally, after what seemed like a maddening forever, she heard Dr. Dressler's voice on the line.

But, by then, Lillian was no longer aware of anything.

Funny, Edie thought absently, rigid and unmoving in one of the blue vinyl chairs aligned around the perimeter of the hospital's brand-new emergency room, she hadn't expected to see Daniel again quite so soon. But at the sight of him hurrying from the parking lot through the automated sliding doors, their last scene was, for the moment, forgotten and she blessed the unerring instinct that had made her dial his number after the ambulance arrived. He put his arms around her and she was comforted by his strength.

"Edie, tell me what happened, everything. You weren't making much sense on the phone. Where is she now?"

She took a deep breath, wiped the tears with what was left of the crumpled tissue in her hand. "In there," she nodded at the swinging doors to the treatment rooms, "with the doctor . . ." Her voice trailed off and she stared, as if willing someone to come through and tell her it was all a terrible mistake.

"Was she conscious?" His questions were relentless. "Was she in pain? Edie, *listen to me*, did she say when it started?"

"What?" She dragged her eyes back to his. "Oh, no. She . . . she looked so terrible when she came home from the movies, and she couldn't talk. And then she, she—" Blindly, Edie slid into one of the chairs, holding her head in her hands, rocking back and forth, tears spilling from between her fingers. "I couldn't do anything for her. Oh Daniel," she looked up suddenly, hands gripping his. "She won't die, w-will she? She's so active, she loves life so *much*, she *can't* die. She can't!" But she knew with chilling certainty that wasn't true and she didn't really expect him to answer.

At that moment the doors swung open and Dr. Dressler came out to them, his steps slow, expression somber. He sat down next to Edie and took her cold hand in his. "Stay with me, kiddo." He put his hand under her chin. "Okay, Edie, here's what's happening. She's had a myocardial infarction—at least one of the arteries to the heart is blocked. Now, I'm a good GP but this is out of my line. There's a pretty good cardiac man down in Cadillac. I called him, and he's on his way."

"How soon will he be here?" The worry on the elderly face rang more alarm bells in her head. "Can you wait?"

He sighed heavily. "We have no choice."

For the first time Daniel spoke. "What are her vitals?" Dr. Dressler looked at him, startled, as if he'd forgotten Daniel was there.

"The BP, pulse, and respiration are okay, for the moment."

"How's the EKG? Can you do a cardiac cath?"

"No, have to wait for the surgeon. She's relatively stable but I'm afraid she may need a balloon pump."

Daniel's worried expression didn't change, only his eyes showed his rising alarm. He shrugged out of his jacket, dropping it on a chair. "I'd like to see her."

"Well, certainly, if . . ." Dr. Dressler glanced at Edie and she nodded quick assent. The two men headed for the doors, Edie following a couple of steps behind.

"No, Edie, wait here."

"Daniel, I'm not a child and I'm not hysterical, so please don't treat me as if I am. I want to be with her."

"Let me look at her first. You know no one is allowed in while a patient's being examined." He tried for calm, reasonable objectivity. It was a response he was used to employing with his patients' families. It enabled them to keep the thread of control intact while they struggled with their fears and uncertainties. Now it served him as well, helping him maintain that facade. Because, of course, this case was different and Edie mustn't see how worried he was.

She knew he was right, and she trusted him to be honest with her. "All right." She held his hand for a second. "Take care of her, Daniel. And please let me know as soon as you—well, let me know." She sank back into the chair, staring blindly at the brightly colored lithographs on the opposite wall as the two men quickly pushed through the doors and disappeared.

Daniel pulled the curtain aside and stepped away from the examination cubicle. He kept his voice low. "How long until Parrini gets here from Cadillac?"

The other man looked at his watch. "Shouldn't be much longer now, if the roads are clear." Suddenly he stared at Daniel. "Say, how do you know it's Parrini? I never mentioned his name."

"He's the only cardiac man in this area who could handle a multiple bypass." Daniel shrugged. "He and I have done some work together."

"Just what kind of surgery do you do, Daniel?" Dr. Dressler looked steadily at him, cautious hope rising. "Are you by any chance a cardiac man?"

"Yeah." The single word was reluctant but resigned.

"Then, in the name of God, why didn't you say—!"

"I don't do surgery anymore." The answer was terse, final.

Dr. Dressler hesitated, then led the way into an empty cubicle, out of the nurses' hearing. "What about an emergency?"

"I haven't held a scalpel in seven months, and I didn't make that decision lightly! Believe me, there are reasons," Daniel said, head down, hands in pockets. "Good reasons."

"Good enough for Lillian Calvin?"

Daniel winced, his face twisting in pain. "That's what I keep asking myself. But I just can't take the chance."

"Dammit Daniel, we all take chances, whenever we cross the street! Doctors take chances every time they diagnose or prescribe." He looked down the hall to the waiting room doors where Edie sat her lonely vigil. "Pharmacists take chances when they fill a prescription. Mothers take chances every time they let their kids walk out the door. There are no guarantees, no sure things."

"I can't operate on her!" Daniel stared down at his hands as if he didn't know why they were there. "Anyway, the hospital's insurance doesn't cover me, I'm not on staff." He'd never have let that stop him, not for Lillian, and Edie. "Look, Parrini is an excellent man and this is a brand-new facility here: he's got the best of everything to work with—"

"The one thing we *don't* have is time."

Daniel muttered a vicious expletive: the older man was right, of course. Some things you can't back away from; some things you can't avoid. That albatross Edie had accused him of clinging to was heavier at this moment than it had ever been.

"Yeah," he sighed, defeated. "Okay. Give him ten more minutes and then I'll scrub. Tell them to get the O.R. ready for bypass. And get George Corey down here." At least George was an experienced surgeon: he'd better have the chief of staff at hand.

"How do you know George? My God, do you know every doctor in the state?" Dr. Dressler smiled, more optimistic somehow than he'd been for a while.

"It helps make up for all the things I *don't* know," Daniel answered wryly and walked toward the waiting room, and Edie.

* * *

"It was lucky Parrini managed to get here in time."
Daniel stood at the foot of Lillian's bed. She was still
pale, still under sedation, and not due to waken for a
few more hours. Edie sat beside the bed, listening to
the rhythmic beeping of the monitoring machines and
watching Lillian's chest rise and fall, breathing regu-
larly and effortlessly now, despite the tangle of tubes
and electrodes protruding from a thick swath of bandages.

"Lucky?" She looked up at him, eyes clear now and
bright with hope. "When you said you'd do the surgery, I was sure she'd make it. You'd have done it
beautifully. I *know* that. I wish you knew it," Edie
murmured, looking back at the bed.

He kept his steady gaze on Lillian's peaceful face
and didn't answer. "She won't regain consciousness
for a while yet. How about a cup of coffee? You look
exhausted."

"Ah, what a way with a compliment!" She smiled
weakly, then nodded and rose from the chair. "But I
could use a shot of caffeine about now." They walked
out and down the hall to the elevator. When they were
seated next to each other in the small, empty basement
cafeteria, she leaned back and looked up at him, expression serious now. "I was glad when you asked permis-
sion to operate." She placed her hand over his beside
the coffee cup. "Of course, I wanted Mom in good
hands, but I was glad for *you*, too."

He stared at her, startled. "Glad for me? What does
that mean?"

"Well, it was a first step, wasn't it?"

He pulled his hand back abruptly. Whatever he felt
he didn't want to hear it said aloud, and definitely not
by her. "It was unavoidable, or at least I thought so. I
didn't know Parrini would get here five minutes later."

"That's exactly what I mean. You were ready to do

it. You made a decision, and you wouldn't have if somehow you didn't *know* you were ready for it.''

"Are you trying to make a point?''

"You've been treading water up here, Daniel, and I—well, I think now you're ready to swim back to shore. Remember, you said you had some thinking to do.'' Lord, was it only a few hours ago? She went on wearily. "Whether or not you realize it, it's just a matter of time until you—'' She couldn't give voice to the last word. Leaving was so final, and her admirable objectivity and calm wouldn't stretch quite that far.

"Until I what? Why should anything change? Edie, why are you looking for obstacles?'' he groaned. He slid the back of his hand along the curve of her throat, along her cheek, wet now with tears. In her eyes he could see the glow of desire, feel her sensitive flesh shivery at his touch.

His strong hands, those life-giving hands, so gentle now, so exciting, lovingly caressed her, and the savage force within her body burst into life again. For a moment her arms crept around his neck, holding him a willing prisoner in her desperate embrace.

"Edie, it will always be this good for us.''

Always. His words brought sanity back with a crushing blow. She pulled back, pushing him away so she could look at him.

"Daniel, how long is 'always'? Can you tell me that—*how long is always, Daniel*?'' She bit off the poignant sob lodged in her throat.

And now it was his turn to pull away, his expression intent. Unmoving, he watched her, the recently absent mask visible again in the bleak metallic gray of his eyes. But he said nothing.

"You can't tell me, can you? Because 'always' is based on *reality*.'' Her words sliced through the cold silence and she slid a few inches across the banquette, putting some distance between them. She had to think clearly now, and so must he.

"And you don't consider this . . . us . . . reality?" He sounded strangely detached, his voice quiet, flat.

"You're talking about selective reality, and that just isn't good enough! Look, Daniel, this time, this place, has been a retreat for you, a refuge. You were hurting, and you needed this. But eventually you must go back. *That's* reality." Edie glanced absently around the still-empty room, then took another swallow of the now lukewarm coffee.

"When I was a little girl, I played a kind of hide-and-seek with my father. When I hid, I'd cover my eyes because, if I couldn't see him then, of course, he couldn't see me either. Well, I'm a big girl now and I've found it doesn't work quite that way. Hell, Daniel, even little four-year-old Brian Detwiler knows that!" She swung back to him, the quiet despair in her voice mirroring the expression flickering behind his eyes. "And someday you'd feel it, too. Better to face it now."

"Do you always know what's best for everyone, or just me?"

"I'm only saying what you know yourself is true. Oh, Daniel, your time up here, what you've discovered about yourself, *whatever* it is, maybe, just *maybe* it's what you've needed, what you sensed was missing before." Edie took a deep breath. "And if it is, don't you *have* to take that chance?"

She couldn't say what she longed to say. That perhaps what he'd found was love, and it would, if he let it, fill up all those empty corners that had haunted him all his life. She couldn't say it because, if it were true, it was something he had to discover for himself, something *he* had to believe.

"You can't build any kind of future on a present that's still filled with doubts and questions. You have

to go back because you have to be sure of the truth.''
Edie blinked and took a deep breath. "I guess we both
have decisions to make.''

But if he goes . . . The empty vistas of her future
didn't bear thinking about. And still, she had to let him
go.

Daniel looked at her, as if memorizing her face,
unable to shut out the quiet relentlessness of her
voice. Edie's words ran ceaselessly through his mind,
like a reel of tape spinning on without end. No matter
how he wanted to refute them he knew she was right.
He'd have no real peace anywhere, ever, if he didn't
stop running and settle it now. That damned
albatross.

"Who would have thought you and Sandra could
have so much in common?" The fatigue in his voice
was bone deep, and endless. "Your logic, like hers, is
absolutely flawless." He hadn't reached sanctuary yet;
he hadn't earned the right to it—yet.

Daniel stared into her eyes a moment more. Suddenly
his jaw flexed, hardened, as her last words echoed in
his thoughts. What was that she'd said about *decisions*?
He turned abruptly, his cynical gray gaze blazing into
her.

"Convenient, too. Now you'll be able to make those
important decisions you're so worried about, without
any more annoying distractions." His voice was hard.
"But I've got to hand it to you, that was very well
done. You almost had me there, with all that," he
sneered, "sincerity."

She stared at him, bewildered, trying to understand,
to ask the right questions. And then it was too late.

With almost frigid indifference Daniel rose briskly
and slipped on his jacket. "This'll give you a good
chance to work out your arrangements with Mr. Mac.
Good luck with your new business. And don't worry,

between Doctor Dressler and George Corey, your mother's in excellent hands.''

He was gone.

He was really gone. *Finis*. Kaput. Back to a world as different from hers as meatloaf from beef Wellington. It was a world she'd once inhabited, a world in which she'd failed, totally and miserably. Edie had never been comfortable or happy there but Mark had wanted it: oh how he'd wanted it! And he'd come to hate her for holding him back. But there was no room for her kind of irreverent honesty, no room for *her*, really. The strange thing was it still stung—oh, how painfully!—knowing she'd been so inadequate, so inept, so out of place.

She sat in the dimly lit hospital room, waiting and thinking. Now she had pushed Daniel back into that same rarefied atmosphere she detested. But it was rightfully his, where he belonged! Money, position, respectability—the novelty of the rural life would pass quickly. He'd have no use for an unregenerate social blasphemer who liked to put her feet on the coffee table and eat chicken and pizza with her bare hands.

She shrugged, self-pity overflowing in great salty tears. Why, really, was she so surprised? She'd beaten him over the head with it, over and over: You have to go back, you can't hide up here forever.

Isn't that wonderful? He agrees with you, you damn fool! You've managed to push him right out of your life. *How long is always, Daniel?* Edie looked into a bleak future and knew she was about to learn the answer.

Well, it wasn't the first time, Daniel thought, slamming the empty dresser drawer. But it would damned well be the last! She'd made her choice. With Mr. Mac's offer of new professional opportunities, it was evident Edie wanted to dispense with—how had Sandra put it?—with being "restricted." But back then, that other time, he hadn't really cared. Now he felt neither numb nor untouched nor indifferent. Now there was anger, and pain.

Thank you, Edie Calvin. You sure taught me how to feel!

Daniel stood at the door for one last moment, looking back at the hushed, dim bedroom, the once cold and sterile room that was now filled with warm memories of her. He saw Edie as she'd been the last time, lying amid the rumpled bedding in wild abandon, joyous and alive and happy, her lovely copper hair spread across his pillow, golden arms reaching up to hold him, to wrap him in delight and desire, to waken a smile on his mouth, tenderness and passion in his heart. He wouldn't ever think of this room, this house, without seeing her. She filled its corners, she filled his mind, his heart . . .

Damn her to hell!

Daniel carried the suitcase down the stairs and left the empty house. He would not be back.

THIRTEEN

In the days that followed she searched valiantly for the old resilient Edie, but she had disappeared. Somewhere in the jumble of belongings Daniel had hurriedly taken from the house by the lake he'd taken *her*, too. Her friends tried their best to help. It wasn't enough. It couldn't be.

Even normally stolid Mr. Mac took to dredging up every old, corny, and downright bad joke he could still remember. Sometimes, inadvertently, he hit a nerve.

"So now," she thought, "I've become a living, breathing joke! 'Did you hear about the gorilla who kidnaps a woman, and when she's finally rescued she becomes despondent thinking about him—he doesn't phone, he doesn't write!' Funny, huh? So, why aren't you laughing?" The red-eyed, pale-faced woman looked back blankly from the mirror; she had no answers, either.

And what's the difference? Edie rationalized. *Daniel couldn't have been happy if he'd stayed up here anyway. And I'd have been rotten at making it down there.*

He didn't ask you, did he?

So then, it's just as well he *didn't* call.

Baloney. Nothing tasted worse than sour grapes.

She turned away, unable to bear the sight of her own hollow eyes, and wandered back down the stairs. It seemed she couldn't find a place for herself in the old house that had always been home and haven. With her mother gone to recuperate at Aunt Essie's, the hours spent at work were her only refuge from loneliness and unanswered questions. *Seems to be my turn to stay in hiding, safe and secure*, and she was more expert on "hiding" than even Daniel had been. He wasn't the only one who knew how to tread water; way past time for her, too, to head for shore.

Easy to solve problems, when they were someone else's problems!

As if on cue, the tinny jingle of the telephone interrupted her futile thoughts. If she didn't call first, her mother called her. Listlessly Edie picked up the receiver.

"Hello, Mom."

"Hello, Edie."

She stared at the receiver and forced herself to breathe.

"Daniel?" she whispered. A tremor of excitement skirled across her shoulder blades. So deep, so quiet, clear, Daniel's voice, that voice she'd heard in her thoughts, her dreams, for five weeks, two days, one hour, and seventeen minutes. But who was counting?

"How . . . how are you, Daniel?" Idiot. What's wrong with: I need you, Daniel—*I love you, Daniel*.

"Fine, Edie," he answered. He hadn't been "fine" since he'd walked out of that hospital room, five weeks, two days, one hour, and eighteen minutes ago. But who was counting!

Of late Daniel wondered frequently if he would ever be "fine" again, but he was well trained and now his voice betrayed nothing.

"I, uh, thought I'd call to see how your mother is doing."

"Mom's doing very well, thank you." She could not *believe* this oh-so-polite conversation! "She's down in Phoenix with Aunt Essie for a few more weeks. Now my aunt can bully her, for a change, and Mom can't fight back." There, that wasn't bad at all. Sounded nice and natural, pretty casual in fact. Just right.

"As long as she's healing well and the doctors are satisfied. Please give her my lo— my best."

Edie had barely managed to keep Lillian innocent of the reason for Daniel's abrupt departure but her excuses had finally seemed to satisfy her mother. "She sent you her . . . love." The last mumbled word was barely discernible.

"And you? How about—?" He stopped, coughed, was silent again. Then, briskly, "So, is everything all settled with the drugstore? I know how important it is to you. When is Mr. Mac leaving?"

For a moment her mind was blank. What did he mean—important? The way he said it, there was something . . . something . . .

She thought back to their last night, and the lights came on. *Revelation!* So that was what he thought: good God, how could he do surgery if he were so blind? Edie spoke slowly, carefully.

"I don't know what I'll be doing—haven't made any plans yet. I told Mr. Mac to look around for someone else, if he can.

She stopped, bit her lip painfully. Didn't he know without him nothing—no plans, no store, *nothing*—held any interest for her now? Even the beloved old house, the town, were no longer the comfortable refuge they'd once been. It was all flat, barren, unimportant. Without him.

"I see."

Did he?

"I left in such a hurry—" He broke off abruptly. "By the way, how are Sarah and my gorgeous little namesake doing? And Lorraine—I really miss that mutt, you know?'' Daniel's low chuckle sent tremors shivering across her skin and she clenched the phone, weak with the heat flooding her veins.

"Sarah and Elizabeth Danielle are doing great. She's gaining weight like crazy.''

"A woman should have some meat on her bones.''

"No, I mean the baby. And she's looking so good Stan says he can't keep his hands off her.''

"The baby.''

"No, *Sarah!*''

They broke into simultaneous laughter, then stopped abruptly. An awkward silence hummed on the line.

"Well . . .'' Edie fumbled for something to say.

"It was . . . good talking to you.''

"Daniel?''

"Yes?'' he answered quickly.

"Er, how are the headaches?''

"Headaches?'' He had to make an effort to remember. "Oh. There aren't any.'' He paused, then said in a very deliberate voice, "You were right, you know . . . about everything.''

She caught her breath at the sharp stab of disappointment. Aah, Edie thought sadly, at last he saw it, too. "Like apples and oranges, I suppose.'' She said it lightly, brightly, the words spilling out in their rush to be said once and for all. "I mean, you'd never want to live up here, any more than . . . than the ridiculous idea that someone like me could be comfortable in your kind of life.'' She didn't wait to hear what he might have said next, for fear of breaking into tears. "Oh, gee, look at the time! I'm sorry Daniel, gotta run, have to take Lorraine out.''

"Yes, certainly,'' he said stiffly. "Tell your mother, and Lorraine and . . . everyone, hello for me. I miss them.'' Quickly he put the receiver back in place, Well, that was that. She couldn't wait to end this call, along with the last remains of their relationship, whatever it had once been, or might have been. She'd said it as plainly as she could—apples and oranges.

The quiet click of his receiver sounded with dull finality in her ear. Mechanically, Edie shrugged on her jacket, pulled on boots, and stoically accompanied Lorraine on her nightly rounds, ending at the dog's favorite tree. Edie realized she hadn't even noticed where they'd walked: her mind had been miles away, at the other end of a disconnected phone line. At least he'd called!

Sure, to check on the local health bulletin.

No, that's only what he said, not what he really meant.

He didn't "really" say anything else.

But he did. By dialing the number. *Her* number, when he could just as easily have called Dr. Dressler. It was there when he said her name, like a sigh, a caress she could feel across her skin. She put a hand on her breast. Even now her body responded, delicious sensation she could never know with anyone but him.

He laughed with you for that one moment, and you know, somehow, it's the first real laughter he's shared since he left. Because only you can do that for him.

The smile on Edie's face, the euphoria in her heart lasted as far as the front door. Slowly doubt and annoyance returned.

". . . your mother . . . Lorraine . . . I miss them." Them? My *mother*? The DOG! "What am I, chopped liver?" This sudden dichotomy between earlier reservations about "his world" and this sudden, inexplicable irritation because he accepted her judgment made her smile in spite of herself. He'd done it again: agreed with her! *Damn him.*

Edie, you dumb bunny, make up your mind . . . you're driving yourself crazy.

Yes, I'm crazy—you're making me crazy, since the first time I set eyes on you!

Oh God, why did she have to remember that now, that perfect afternoon, the firelit bronze of his beautiful body, the touch of his hand gliding, stroking? She could taste him, even now, feel the supple strength of muscle rippling and flexing beneath the skin when her hands finally held him.

Edie felt the dull, heavy throbbing in her body, her very core trembling with the memory of him, of that day and the others they'd shared, the desire and the perfect completeness that had been theirs. She'd been *whole* then.

And she would never be that way again.

Hell, she was right about that, too!

Tears boiled over at last: after all, it was for the best they part, separated by time and distance and circumstance. She'd known, but his voice had unleashed despair she couldn't deny.

When the storm of weeping finally wore itself out, Edie lay exhausted in the darkness, her mind still a tangle of emotions.

Dear God, she missed him so! And hearing his voice had made it worse. Because, loving him, there was no peace for her, not here, not anywhere. It didn't matter where she was, what she did—if he wasn't there, nothing else mattered.

He'd sounded so sad, so alone, so—

Edie sat bolt upright.

Oh, my. Love really is blind!

In disgust, she brushed away the last remnant of tears: no time for *that*. She felt a burst of buoyant energy, a newborn determination. She positively sparkled. She glowed!

She packed.

"Oh, all right, all *right*! I'm coming!" Three o'clock in the morning, for God's sake, and some damn fool had his finger grafted to the door buzzer. "Who is it?"

"Me!"

One word, and all he needed. Daniel threw open the door, only to find himself under attack on two fronts. An irresistible pressure on his chest forced him backward into the room, while something wrapped itself around his legs, immobilizing him from any strategic resistance.

"I'm sick and tired of all this stupidity!" Edie was in her attack mode. "You forgot something in that little phone call, didn't you? Well, *didn't you*? Of course you did. And a careful man like you doesn't forget things—not *you*. So, what you didn't say you didn't say deliberately, just to annoy me, I'll bet. Well, dammit, I'm annoyed! Shut your mouth, Daniel, you look like a dying goldfish with it hanging open like that." Edie pulled Lorraine after her into the spacious riverfront apartment, still poking a finger into Daniel's bare chest. Dumbfounded, and nimbly managing to avoid tripping over what he recognized as Lorraine's leash, he retreated across the wide expanse of thickly carpeted floor, forced backward in the face of Edie's intrepid advance.

"Let me tell you something, Daniel. I *need* you, and believe me, I'm not comfortable *needing* anyone! My only consolation is that you need me, too . . . whether or not you know it, *you do*! But that's okay, as long as *I* know it. And mister, *I do*! What's wrong, you suddenly run out of words? Can't weasel out of it? Well, it's too late anyway. Oh sure, you called after all this time to ask about my mother. In a pig's eye, you did. You could have called the doctor. But you *didn't*—you called *me*!"

Edie took a deep breath. Daniel stood there, a foolish grin on his face: before he could speak, she was off and running again.

"So, you just listen to me, Doctor Daniel James Slayton the Third! *If* you don't care about me, *and* you don't miss me, *and* you don't need me, then you just tell me to my face, right now! 'Cause I drove a lot of miles to see you and, you turkey, you'd better say *something* . . ."

She could't stop; she was scared to death and fighting for her life. "I know I don't belong in your kind of life, I won't fit in. Oh, but Daniel, if that's what you want, I'll try." Her voice cracked as her motor ran down and he thought he saw her chin quiver. "I really will! And I'll *do* it, you'll see. I did it once, well almost, and I'll get it right this time!"

"Edie—"

"The 'simple life' was so dull and empty when you weren't around. And I realized *where* I was had nothing to do with being alive, really alive! What mattered was who I was alive *with*. I finally had to face the truth, no matter how I tried to avoid it. Now *that's* something you ought to be able to understand— avoidance."

"But Edie—"

"And I don't give two hoots and a holler about that drugstore and owning my own business and being outstanding in my profmmph—"

"Edie, shut up." He put his hand on her mouth, gentle fingers tracing her parted lips, and like blank windows in an empty house coming alive with the first light of dawn, Daniel's eyes reflected new dreams.

"You once told me you couldn't talk and kiss at the same time." His slow smile grew wider and brighter across his face. "So start kissing." He didn't wait, couldn't wait, so desperate was he to fill his arms with her again, to taste her sweet, warm skin, her hair, the smooth, soft body responding under his touch, not the taunting will-o'-the-wisp of too many restless dreams.

"Oh Lord, Edie, I've missed you! More than my stupid, stubborn, senseless pride would admit." His mouth devoured her, almost brutally, and it was a savagery she reciprocated. They strained together in a fierce contest of passion, nothing held back now, needing to erase the awful loneliness.

"I'm terribly . . . overdressed for . . . the . . . occasion," she murmured in an unsteady whisper while he discarded her coat and sweater, interrupting only for a moment her fingers busy on the cord of his low-slung silk pajamas.

"Where there's a will . . ." Daniel muttered between kisses along her neck and over her shoulder. She shivered at the touch, then shed the last of her clothing in a frenzied impatience to feel his body against her own, nothing between them but the heat of their desire. She ached to feel him inside her, part of her. Dear heaven, she needed to be whole again.

"How many dreams ago did I hold you like this?" Daniel slid his hands up her arms, so close nothing on earth could have torn her away from him.

Edie gazed into the face that had become so precious to her. Her hands, locked around his waist, stroked his back, the tense cords of muscle beneath the smooth sheath of skin. She exulted in the sheer joy of touching him, at last.

"Mmm, you feel so good! Until this moment I didn't realize how much I missed you." Edie's hands slid over his shoulders, the smooth expanse of his chest. *Oh but she had known, had ached for weeks with the knowing!*

A tremor shot through him as her fingers rubbed lightly over the flesh and she leaned forward to kiss the path they had taken. The moist darting of her tongue and her gentle bites on the sensitive skin were the final test for Daniel's control.

She grinned agreement, raised her arms to his neck, and rested her head against his straining chest. He half-carried her down the hall into his bedroom, her mouth cherishing the warm flesh under her lips. His pulse beat loudly beneath her ear, and she gloried in the knowledge of his response to her.

Because her reaction to his caresses was just as wild. "Daniel, Daniel, do you know what you do to me? All that hard-won maturity and sophistication—shot to hell!"

As one, complete and perfect, they fell to the bed, the rumpled sheets still warm from his body, where she'd so abruptly roused him from an unsatisfying, restless sleep. Where he touched her, Edie felt her skin begin to glow and tingle, as if hundreds of tiny fireworks were exploding across the surface, warm and vibrant, scattering a million stars over her body. She was wrapped in a shimmery net of sensation, rising to new heights with every stroke of his hands, every touch of his lips, every sweet caress of his tongue.

To one who is starving, restraint at a banquet table is impossible. So it was for Edie and Daniel. Too long denied they couldn't hold back. And why should they? They had come home, where they belonged . . . together.

Daniel rose before Edie, quietly, not disturbing her. She looked so young, so sweet, so desirable. He resisted the impulse to stay there with her and instead slipped into his clothes and took a long-patient Lorraine downstairs for a predawn walk. Along the waterfront path that edged the Detroit river behind the tall shaft of the elegant apartment building, thin rays of sunlight struggled to push through leaden clouds and both man and dog were happy to come back to the warmth of the sanctuary on the top floor. Daniel crawled back beneath the welcoming covers, curling instinctively into Edie's body, and slept the sleep of a thoroughly contented man. It was mid-afternoon before he and Edie were finally able to talk.

"What was all that before about 'belonging' and 'fitting in'?" He was sprawled across her limp body, lazily tracing her form with one finger while the other hand possessively cupped her breast just under his cheek. His eyes were closed and a small, satisfied smile of completion rested on his mouth.

"Hmmm?" Edie was content to stay where they were, if not forever, then for at least an eternity or two. His finger was teasing the hardened tip of her breast and she only wanted to lap up the delicious sensation. "Oh. Well, Daniel . . ." she sighed, "you . . . you . . . mmmm!"

"I what?" His low chuckle reverberated outward through her body from his resting place on her belly, sending shivery quakes down her spine, bathing her in a warm haze.

"You know, the life you live, the kind of people you associate with, all this . . ." Her languid gesture included the spacious penthouse apartment, its garden terrace visible beyond the uncurtained window wall. "It's not exactly Tobacco Road."

"It isn't the Garden of Eden, either. The 'life' I live? What life? This is a *place*, not a life. Edie, *you* gave me life. And you 'belong' anywhere! Anywhere you want to belong." She heard the question under his determined answer.

"Oh Daniel, I *want*, I want you—I'm afraid I want too damn much. But I don't know, a sow's ear makes a pretty shabby silk purse."

He grinned. "Who you calling a sow's ear? Listen, you gorgeous thing, you're *my* silk purse. I'd put my valuables in you anytime. As a matter of fact," he arched his brows, "I already have . . . on several memorable occasions." He rubbed his hand over her hip, her navel, resting, as if by natural right, on the shadowy russet tangle below. "Mmmm, softer than silk, too." He rested his cheek on the pillow of her stomach, his gentle breath fluttering across the flesh and the moist nest of copper curls.

The tide of sensation rushed through her again, intense and bubbling and drowning out every doubt and confusion that hid in her heart.

Daniel never tired of exploring the depth of his desire for her. And hers for him. He would never be used to the wonder of it. His finger touched one of the springy little curls, combing gently through. He was so close he could see the gooseflesh spring up on her skin, feel the sharp quiver of response under his cheek.

"Daniel! Ohhh, I can't . . . can't think when . . . you do that . . . !"

"Good," he murmured. "There are times, my sexy little mad scientist, when thinking is absolutely unnecessary . . . and this is one of— *Son of a*—!"

For one wild moment he entertained the thought of ripping the offending telephone out of the wall and tossing it through the window into the Detroit River far below. Then sanity returned and he rolled over, answering with an admirably calm and professional manner. "Hello?"

Suddenly the temperature of his voice dropped several noticeable degrees. "No, Mother, I haven't forgotten. Seven *sharp*." He glanced at Edie snuggling innocently into the covers and a look of dangerous determination appeared on his face. "By the way, set another place. That's right, a friend." Edie's head jerked up in sudden alarm, shaking emphatic negatives at him, answered by his own equally emphatic nods as he abruptly hung up the phone.

With annoyance and fear lending equal heat to her furious glare, Edie armored herself in the folds of the sheet wrapped tightly around her.

"I take it I'm the 'friend.' " He nodded once. "Well, this may just be the end of our beautiful friendship. I don't . . . I'm not ready for . . . She . . ."

"How articulate." He raised one dark eyebrow in disbelief. "Why, Edith Stephanie Calvin, you're afraid!"

"Meet your newest convert—just another devout coward."

"Who's playing hide-and-seek now?" His quiet voice crystallized all her obscure and nebulous fears. "Someone—a pretty smart someone—once told me you can't turn your back on a problem and pretend it doesn't exist, that you have to face it."

"What idiot told you that?" Edie muttered. She was not exactly gracious in defeat. And it was defeat. What sensible argument could she offer? She knew he was right, and he knew she knew.

Did he also know how very frightened she really was?

"Now, where were we when we were so rudely interrupted?"

Damn, he was so disgustingly smug! "Oh no, you don't. If you're so determined to push me into the lions' den I need time to get my armor in shape."

"Your shape looks good enough to me," he leered.

"Yeah, well, ''good enough' isn't good enough. Not for tonight." Edie thought of Daniel's mother. Not for *that* lion.

Two hours later she stared into the mirror at The Dress. She'd bought it at Neiman Marcus in Chicago, on a whim and a sale, but it had waited, unworn, for a special occasion that never came. Somehow, the divorce hearing had hardly seemed appropriate. Edie had brought it with her, on the chance that her meeting with Daniel would prove to be very special indeed.

And now it was Zero Hour. Go for broke. Because, after all, this was why she was here—to prove, maybe to herself more than him, that she could share some small part of his life. And there would never be a more acid test than Amanda Slayton.

At the sound of her footsteps Daniel rose eagerly from his chair. "I was beginning to give up hope! What . . . took . . . ?" The half-formed question died on his lips and he stood staring at the stunning vision poised beside the sofa.

Well! Whatever it cost and however long I waited to wear it, it's certainly worth it!

Daniel had never seen Edie like this, never pictured her in the sophisticated Chicago scene she'd been part of for so long, never came close to imagining. She was exquisite. The carelessly tumbled curls lay now in a smooth crescent angling over her eyes, then swept behind her ears in a lustrous coppery coil. It was caught to one side by a beautiful antique clasp encrusted with myriad seed pearls set in graceful flower-shaped clusters amid the dull gold filigree.

Artfully applied makeup enhanced the flush of nervous excitement on her cheeks, and the amber glitter sparking her wide eyes reflected the quiet gleam of delicate gold and pearl earrings. Darkened lashes lent a subtle touch of mystery to the intensity of the gaze she returned to him; her mouth gleamed moist and red as she drew air anxiously through half-parted lips.

Edie worked nervous hands up and down the sides of the fabric gently sheathing her hips. A slim, straight column of black velvet, long, tight-fitted sleeves, and an unrelieved square neckline slashing low across the swelling curve of her breasts. A stark, deceptive simplicity revealed the understated elegance of cut and line, a perfect foil for pale skin and glowing hair. She wore it with an inherent air of ease and sophistication.

"Daniel? Please, *say* something—anything!" Oh God, she was a fool. She'd thought she could be Cinderella: she was more like one of the stepsisters and he was too polite to tell her.

"Edie, you look—!" His voice was almost reverent. "What in the name of God were you worried about? You could outshine a duchess."

"Well, you don't have to sound *quite* so surprised, you know," she teased, relief and love sweeping over her. "But thank you, I needed that! Because inside this duchess beats the quivering heart of a chicken." She peered at him, unconvinced. "Seriously, will I do?"

"Oh yes, you'll do just fine!" As if he'd ever had any doubts. His soft silver eyes, his warm and tender kiss, told her what he saw, what he felt. All she ever needed to know. His deep voice was quiet with emotion and pride. "How about magnificent?"

"Oh! Well, magnificent will do very nicely, thank you."

When it came to magnificent, she thought, he was way out of her league. The man had a patent on "magnificent." He wore his perfectly tailored navy suit with an elegance a male model would have envied, although it wasn't something Daniel would ever try to cultivate. The fresh white of the silk shirt and the conservative perfection of the richly patterned burgundy silk tie blended with the subtle burgundy pinstripe in the suit. Edie allowed herself a few seconds of quiet pleasure watching him. Something reached out and grabbed hold of her heart. No one should ever love anyone this much!

"I promise it will be a short evening. One of these every six months or so is all I can take anyway. And besides, I've got a late date with a 'good friend.' " He winked and opened the door with a flourish. She began to button her coat as they walked to the elevator.

That's when they heard it. Quite possibly the entire building heard it.

It began with a low, monotonous whine, then rose in a spiraling crescendo from behind the closed door until it filled the spacious hallway. It gained strength as it ricocheted from wall to wall, echoing and re-echoing with a horrifying screech that could be heard in every apartment on the floor, and all those below. Thank God there weren't any above.

"Good God!" Daniel stopped in his tracks. "What the hell is that?"

Edie bit her lip, and didn't feel the pain. "I, uh, I think it's . . . Lorraine."

They stared at each other in consternation, having completely forgotten the dog in their hurry to leave. On their quick reentrance to the apartment, it didn't take long to prove that no amount of food, water, or leg lifting on the terrace would placate Sweet Lorraine's ruffled canine feelings.

"My kingdom for ice cream and a beer," Edie moaned. The long car trip, the strange surroundings, and the ignominy of total abandonment, first by Lillian and then by her beloved Edie and Daniel, were just too much for Lorraine's delicate sensibilities.

"Well, I guess you'd better go on ahead without me, Daniel. I'll just stay here with her." Edie didn't sound terribly disappointed.

Daniel shook his head stubbornly. "Talk about weaseling out of something! No, I have a much better idea. We'll just take her with us. She can either stay in the car—"

"She'll freeze!"

"—or we can tie her up in the kitchen pantry during

dinner. She won't be alone, there's plenty of food, and ice cream, and we can run out and see her every now and then.''

A smart man, Daniel. But this time he was wrong. It wasn't one of his better ideas.

FOURTEEN

The house's imposing pseudo-Greek columns and ornate brickwork and granite were a masterpiece of intimidation.

"What time does the tour leave?" Edie whispered with a bravado that barely covered her panic.

Just then the door swung open; a stern-faced man bowed and ushered them in. His demeanor cracked visibly when he saw what was on the end of the leash. Eyebrows leaped to fill the void left by a receding hairline, but he didn't utter a word: he didn't need to. His pale eyes showed disapproval and Edie quickly nudged Daniel to end the suffocating silence.

"Phillips, this is Miss Calvin."

Edie thought that wasn't the best news of Phillips' day.

"Good evening, Miss." He bowed, eyes never leaving the offending presence of Miss Calvin's four-legged friend.

"We'll leave the dog in the pantry until after dinner," Daniel explained.

Phillips blanched.

The small procession moved to the designated area,

all but ignored by the kitchen staff. Daniel was so seldom in the house he'd become merely another temporary presence, to be treated with deference but meriting no further concern.

For Edie the moment of truth arrived too soon. How long could you attend to a dog bent on closing her eyes and drifting off into her usual stupor? Sure, *now* she was sleepy!

"It's time, Edie," Daniel warned reluctantly. "I'll tell one of the staff to give her some food and ice cream when she wakes." He did so, and the harried maid promptly forgot.

They returned to the foyer and into the huge room beyond. Six other people stood talking to each other, a Mozart concerto emanating from hidden speakers, background filler for any gaps in the conversation. The presence of the two newcomers was noted and thoroughly observed. Later, Edie hardly remembered her stiff smile and repeated hellos as Daniel steered her through the perfectly appointed elegance of the room. A vague familiarity bothered her, more sensed than seen, more evocative than real . . . until she realized it was merely the stately elder sister of the house by the lake, as it had been when she first met Daniel.

She shivered now as she had then.

Once, Daniel had seen Edie as the source of light and warmth and color in that other house. And now she was introduced to the source of the coldly sterile beauty of this one.

"Mother, this is Edie Calvin. Edie, my mother, Amanda Slayton." That voice, flat and cold and totally devoid of personal inflection, reserved only for his mother.

She was a striking woman. Silver hair streaked with the same dark shade as Daniel's framed a beautiful but rigid face, frozen into a permanent state of disapproval.

Tiny lines around eyes and mouth marked the passage of the years.

They weren't laugh lines, Edie thought.

The woman's bearing was regal: she'd be the center of any gathering. The straight shaft of her back supported a strong, slender neck and creamy, still shapely shoulders displayed above the elegant drape of her gown. A diamond choker circled her throat, appearing to give added support to the imperious tilt of her head, and almost covered the crepey skin that testified to the inroads of age. Even she, Edie was amused to note, was prey to the demands of vanity. But—a woman to be reckoned with.

An expressive rise of haughty brows; an impatient glance at the ormolu clock on the mantel, two minutes past the hour; the pursed mouth; and an icy glance: they were late.

"How do you do, Edith? That is your name, I trust? I do detest these slovenly diminutives so prevalent in some circles."

Delightful. Slovenly diminutives were evidently on par with sloppy sentimentality. Amanda Slayton exerted all the charm of Attila the Hun.

"Yes, my friends use Edie. You may call me Edith." Good Lord, she hadn't meant it quite that way. Had she? Yes, she had.

It seemed to pass right over the older woman's head. "And have you known my son very long?"

"No, just for a couple of months." She looked at Daniel. *Just all my life.*

Amanda's eyes widened. "You mean you live up in . . . what *is* the name of that village you ran off to, Daniel?"

Daniel's hand tightened convulsively on Edie's arm and she felt his anger increasing by the second. Amanda's rudeness was not, as Edie had thought, deliberate. It was worse. It was instinctive, spontaneous. An utterly insensitive human being, she realized sadly. And what damage she had done.

"I'm sure you've never heard of Pecomish Springs," Edie answered with saccharine sweetness. She took Daniel's right hand and held it up, palm forward, as most Michiganians do, using the state's unique mitten shape for illustration. She caressed the base of his thumb lightly, provocatively, running a bright red fingernail slowly across the skin and up the length of his pinkie. Tension made his hand rigid: she must remind him to laugh instead of boil. "Danny boy has a lovely summer home up there." Edie smiled innocently as he choked at the name.

At that instant they were distracted by the jingle of the filled wineglasses on the tray Phillips was carrying through the room. For a moment it shook in his hand and Edie surprised a faint gleam of quiet satisfaction in his eyes before he turned to the other guests. Amanda continued to maintain her steady gaze at Edie and Daniel, though her color flared for an instant.

"I see!" A white-lipped Amanda frowned angrily and quickly sipped wine from the Waterford crystal goblet in her perfectly manicured hand. Abruptly she changed tactics.

"Your dress is quite . . . lovely."

The compliment was negated by the acid tone of contempt: *The country bumpkin must have bought it to impress her betters.*

"Why, thank you. I bought this the year I was Miss Michigan Swine." Edie smiled graciously; somewhere behind her she heard what sounded suspiciously like a stifled giggle amid the quiet social chatter of the other guests.

Amanda seemed to shrivel as Edie waxed ever more enthusiastic, fired by the memory of pain in Daniel's eyes when he spoke of this woman. "Came in handy when I officiated at the supermarket openings and 4-H banquet. We've a couple of new restaurants, even salad bars and *cloth napkins*! Haven't had to wipe my hands on a tablecloth in a long time. Oh, we've made such progress!''

Amanda's mouth grew thinner, her posture rigid. Her son, on the other hand, suddenly felt marvelous, as he never had before in this house. He relished the sight of the redoubtable Amanda Slayton giving ground to the redheaded upstart from the north. Edie didn't need protection—she was doing just fine on her own.

"I see that *progress* has not extended to good manners and respect for your elders."

Aha! Daniel knew that tone, if the others did not. It was a measure of Amanda's discomfort that she seemed oblivious to the other ears in the vicinity, all tuned to the same frequency. Daniel struggled to restrain the grin tugging at his lips.

"I apologize. I was taught to always respect others, as I would wish them to respect me." The quiet dignity of Edie's answer left her speechless hostess grateful for Phillips' timely arrival in the doorway to announce dinner. They all moved at once, breaking the curious hush that had fallen over the room.

Beneath the glittering crystal canopy of a huge chandelier Edie found herself seated beside an elderly gentleman she vaguely recalled being introduced to as a Mr. Chapin. His spare frame was the single and, Edie feared, inadequate buffer between her and her hostess. Across the broad lace-covered table, through a forest of candles and wineglasses, Daniel, on his mother's left, offered Edie a smile of encouragement. It was not lost on a frozen-faced Amanda, whose grim expression augured no good.

Edie weakly returned his smile but, proper gentleman that he was, she knew he was merely making the best of a very bad situation. Damn, how could she have behaved like that? There were no excuses—she was a *guest* in this house! Her mother would kill her if she knew. She bit her lip, resolved to try harder. She'd bite her tongue right out of her *head* before she made one more rude remark—no matter how well deserved!

From then on Edie devoted herself diligently to chatting with Mr. Chapin, whose admirable good nature kept her wondering how he'd ever made it onto Amanda's guest list. His laughter, loud and frequent, was a testament to his delight in Edie's company. It did nothing to endear either of them to Amanda.

The woman did get points for perseverance, Edie thought wryly, as the evening proceeded. Whenever a conversational gap reared its unwanted head she was there, innuendos and probes undiminished. Any resemblance between Amanda Slayton and Torquemada, Edie decided, was more than superficial.

But eventually even Amanda had to withdraw and regroup: Edie's defenses were impregnable. She slid past the first course, asparagus bisque, with deceptive ease, using the correct spoon and not slurping once, hardly mindful at that point of the faint whine in the distance. Sirens were, after all, not uncommon along the night streets of a city.

"Daniel." Amanda now trained her sights on him. "The Art Institute Founders' Society preview of the Rodin exhibit is tomorrow night. I assume you will be there." She turned to Edie and her cool smile ill concealed a gleam of triumphant anticipation in her cold eyes. "Are you familiar with Rodin's work?" clearly implying the possibility was utterly beyond imagination.

Before her more polite alter ego could speak, some perverse devil compelled Edie's deliberately obtuse answer. "Rodan? Oh yes," she enthused, "I've seen every movie with Rodan, and Godzilla, too! The Japanese have such a unique approach to the horror movie, don't you think?" She beamed ingenuously around the table as six heads turned to her and six baffled faces stared their bewilderment. Amanda looked lost. Daniel, shoulders shaking, closed his eyes and bit his lips together.

The opportune arrival of the next course was silently welcomed by an increasingly unsettled hostess. The rack of lamb was delicious, and uneventful, save Amanda's stare when Daniel deliberately picked up a bone and began to nibble with diligence.

"Your manners have deteriorated." The determined, rigid smile on her thin lips hardly moved with the venomous whisper. "You didn't learn that at *this* table."

"I didn't learn much of real value at this table, Mother." His quiet words were meant for her ears alone. "But," he gestured with the bone, his voice at conversational level once more, "I've found the meat next to the bone is sweeter."

Edie gulped, recalling where and when he'd learned that. Daniel smiled, a wide, innocent smile, directly at his mother, and she blinked, dazed. This was a Daniel quite unknown to her, and she was stunned as he added, "Life is a banquet. We have to taste it all, while we can." And, placidly, he went on gnawing.

Dessert, at last, was served. A grateful Edie had feared the meal, like a scene in an existential hell, might go on forever. *If I can survive this night, I can survive anything! My teeth must be ground down to the gums by now!* She began to eat the velvety dark chocolate mousse floating on a pool of custard sauce heartily redolent of rum and vanilla. One thing she had to credit Amanda with: she had a great cook.

The rising decibel level of a distant siren continued relentlessly, becoming more annoying and intrusive to the conversation at the table. The noise suddenly ascended to a loud, mournful howling resounding and echoing through the spacious high-ceilinged rooms. From the direction of the kitchen came a crash, loud slams, excited voices . . . and a queer click-click-click advancing across the marble floor of the foyer.

"Oh my God." Edie, at least, recognized that sound.

A fuzzy, furry missile suddenly catapulted across the magnificent Aubusson rug toward the most familiar face in this strange room full of strange people: Edie. Unfortunately, a more desirable target presented itself en route. Amanda, at the head of the table, had paused at the intrusion, her vanilla custard-laden spoon raised halfway to her lips.

It really wasn't Lorraine's fault. On the other hand, it wasn't really Edie's fault either. And could you honestly blame Daniel? Well, of course, it must be Amanda's *own* fault—who told her to serve French vanilla *anything* anyway?

The lady in question recoiled in horror at that moment, as a hairy brown rocket launched itself with miraculous effort, sadly unappreciated, off the floor and into her lap, burying its face ecstatically in the dessert dish. Doggy heaven!

Edie cringed. And if Edie was in shock, Amanda was catatonic, her de la Renta–covered lap full of basset hound. The rest of the dinner guests were caught in varying stages of turmoil ranging from wide-eyed distaste through shock to gleefully unconcealed amusement. The hapless kitchen staff huddled frozen in the doorway, too startled to move, too smart to laugh.

Throughout all the chaos and confusion, the focus of all this untoward activity perched contentedly, blissfully unperturbed, her vanilla-sauced canine face showing a foolish smile of total ecstasy.

In the sudden stunned silence the only sound was a queer gasping accompanied by a series of strangled coughs. Edie was too humiliated to even notice, but a rapidly unraveling Amanda turned to find Daniel, one hand trying vainly to smother his laughter and streaming eyes behind a crumpled dinner napkin, the other pounding the table in unrestrained glee at the utter shambles that had descended on the once staid and decorous room.

"Get . . . rid of . . . this . . . this . . . *this*!" Amanda's just short of hysterical fury was an icy whiplash across the room.

Edie leapt from her chair. They couldn't hit a moving target, she reasoned. Pulling a now tranquil, semisatisfied Lorraine from Amanda's lap, Edie coiled the dragging leash around her hand to forestall further raids on the dessert. She grabbed her delicate lace napkin to mop up Lorraine's face and paws. The voice of Amanda Slayton cut like a buzz saw.

"Don't let us detain you! Take that animal back where it belongs. *And leave the table linen.*"

Cheeks flaming with embarrassment, Edie halted, carefully folded the napkin, and placed it on the table. "I—I apologize. For everything. As a guest in your house my bad manners were unforgivable." Blinking back tears she stared at the leash coiled tightly in her hand. "As for the dog, that was . . . an unfortunate mistake. But it's just as well. You're right, Mrs. Slayton. I *will* take her back where she belongs, where we both belong. It certainly isn't here, I know that. I'm sure everyone knows it." She fought the sick, empty feeling in the pit of her stomach.

She dared one last look at Daniel. "I'm so sorry. I thought, because I love . . . that maybe . . ." Edie's voice dropped to a choked whisper, breaking. "Goodbye, Daniel."

She wheeled suddenly and hurried blindly from the room. The leash cut cruelly into her hand, but not as cruelly as the horrid scene cut into her heart. Edie snatched her coat from the hands of a strangely sympathetic-looking Phillips and rushed out the front door. She hit the ground running and never looked back.

* * *

"Daniel!"

He stopped, busy whispers rustling in the room around him.

"Where do you think you're going?"

He looked at Amanda with cool, clear eyes. "I *know* where I'm going, Mother. I'm getting out of this beautiful mausoleum and rejoining the land of the living! Good-bye."

A second later he stuck his head back around the door. "Send the cleaning bills to me. I'm used to them by now." With that puzzling remark he followed the other two escapees.

Silence descended around the littered remains of the elegant dinner. Utter, uncomfortable, unbroken silence.

The door opened again, and Phillips advanced across the carpet to Amanda's chair, a small silver tray in his neatly white-gloved hand. He silently offered her the single glittering tumbler it bore. Without a word she lifted it to her lips and swallowed, without the blink of an eye, a double scotch—neat.

A car pulled to the curb and the door swung open, blocking her path. For a moment Edie panicked, then recognized the silver Jaguar. The alternative might have been preferable.

"Get in. Don't argue! Just get in."

Hell, where were all the muggers when you needed one?

The ride back to his apartment was accomplished in unbroken silence. Even Lorraine sensed the tension. She didn't lick Daniel's hand once.

"I'll leave as soon as I change," Edie mumbled, brushing past him in her flight to the bedroom. Lorraine, *the miserable traitor*, ignoring the hand that would from now on feed her—*if she was lucky!*—had stayed with Daniel in the other room. Edie stripped off dress and hose—it'd be a cold day *anywhere* before she wore it again!—and pulled on jeans and T-shirt, tears flowing quietly down her pale cheeks. She was tossing things into her suitcase before she actually heard the music from the other room.

Music? *Her heart was broken, she wanted to crawl away and die . . . and he was playing dance music.* Oh, how could he! She went to slam the door shut. And then she began to listen.

Her steps slowed and, like a sleepwalker, she walked into the living room. Daniel slouched in the large over-stuffed white chair, hands behind his head, legs out-stretched, in a posture of unruffled relaxation. Tie and jacket were gone and his eyes were closed, a beatific smile stretched across his mouth.

"I never knew you liked that song," Edie breathed shakily.

Daniel opened one eye. "Mmm, one of my favorites." His low voice shivered down her spine. He closed the eye, still smiling.

Edie stared at him, not daring to breathe, not daring to hope. As if sensing her look, he raised his eyes in a sizzling silver gaze. Slowly he opened his arms to her and she moved hesitantly into his embrace. He folded her in his waiting arms and held her close, cradled on his lap. They sat cuddled tightly together and listened to the husky velvet voice of Nat 'King' Cole singing about his "Sweet Lorraine."

Daniel's hands moved across her body. He was not, she noted dreamily, nearly as relaxed as he appeared. Edie felt him hardening, swelling beneath her even as she snuggled closer.

"Don't you want to wait until he finishes singing?" Daniel teased, nibbling delicately on her ear.

"I'd wait for you as long as you want, Daniel," she murmured hoarsely, "as long as it's not too long!"

Delicious spasms of anticipation and desire were shuddering uncontrollably through her body.

"That T-shirt has given me a wonderful idea," Daniel whispered in her ear, a butterfly breath sending goose-bumpy shivers up her spine. She glanced down at the shirt she'd grabbed: "I may not be perfect . . . but parts of me are excellent." His fingers teased gently at her erect, swollen breasts, impudently visible through the soft cotton knit.

"Oh Lord, I always knew I'd be in trouble if I ever went braless." *Mmmm, some trouble!*

"I have this sudden urge—"

"I'm a sucker for your sudden urges," she sighed.

"—this sudden urge," his fingers moved deliberately, "to check all those parts. You know, to see how excellent they are."

He moved his hand gently up the side of her throat and lifted the soft copper mass of loosed hair. The elusive caress of his lips bathed the fragile flesh at the nape of her neck with a sweet, moist kiss. The gentleness of that kiss was deceptive, the torrent of desire it let loose as powerful as a river at full flood. And she was swept up in it, with no more will than a leaf caught in its relentless current. A delicious lassitude stole over her as his mouth and hands caressed her.

Daniel's hand slipped up the warm, moist valley between her breasts, pulling the hem of the thin shirt until all of her upper body was bared to his sight, cradled in his arms, inviting him to share its silken secrets. He drew one erect rosy crest into the heat of his mouth and his tongue paid loving homage, telling her how very precious she was. The soft mewling purr low in her throat answered him. She was incapable of words.

When Daniel lifted her in his arms and rose from the chair, she was hardly aware, not until she felt the cool sheet slide under the fevered skin of her back. Edie made an ineffectual attempt to rid herself of the jeans but he stopped her.

"No, love. Let me." The low intensity of his voice and the fire of his hands stilled her. Very slowly, almost gently, he pulled the zipper and peeled them down her legs. He slipped off her shirt and lifted her arms to the pillow under her head. And for a brief moment he sat beside her in the dimly lit room, his hand gliding softly over her body, looking at her as she lay there, still in that dreamy, languid state. His eyes and his fingers traced an adoring trail over her body, across her face.

Tenderly, Daniel closed her eyelids, then ran his fingers over the ridge of her brows, her nose, cupping her cheek while he dipped his head to place a gentle kiss there. His large hands caressed with a feather touch the soft line of her jaw. Now, tonight, he needed to show her the enchantment, the delight she had given him. His own pleasure and release he could subdue a while longer because it was so intricately, intimately bound up with hers. Her joy would be his, her pleasure his. And as it swelled and flowered, so would his. He knew that . . . though he'd never before felt this sense of glorious unity . . . he knew it with a primal instinct that had no conscious thought. The man he was tonight bore no resemblance to the man he once had been.

Daniel's hands slipped across Edie's supple skin and with the tips of his fingers shadowed a path to the fullness of her breasts, waiting impatiently for his touch. He covered them, filling his hands with her sweet, soft flesh, sending tremors of desire through her body.

Caught in the hypnotic tranquility of the magical moment Edie raised heavy-lidded eyes. That expression on his face!—it defied description. But the faint gleam of tears she saw in the corners of his eyes told her what words could never have said.

"Somewhere, sometime, I must have done something very good."

His choked whisper only crystallized the incoherent and unformed chaos of her own thoughts. Edie lifted her hand and laid it atop his, still fondling her breast.

"Ah, Daniel," she sighed, a dreamy smile on her lips. "You didn't have to do anything but be you. That was enough, that was always enough."

No one, in all his lonely life, had ever told him that, given him cause to think it. It had never occurred to him that it could be true. Edie saw it in the wondering gaze he gave her, the tender smile as he looked at her with his heart in his eyes.

Love shone from those silver eyes of his, love and trust. *Trust.* She could trust him, trust her own feelings for him . . . his for her. And so every other fear was meaningless.

Daniel's hands cherished her, his mouth woke exquisite excitement, and Edie thought—if she was capable of thought at all—that if this were the last sensation her body could know on this earth, it would be worth all the rest.

Her blood hummed with a pulsing vibration. Splinters of light darted through her veins, bringing to fiery life erotic areas she hadn't suspected. She began to move restlessly, feverishly, clenching and unclenching her fists in the tangled sheet, and the spiraling ecstasy whirled through her blood.

Her skin gleamed opalescent, covered with a fine sheen of perspiration, and deep within him Daniel knew, at last he *knew* . . . she was his, all her sweetness, kindness, and laughter, her passion and love . . . his! As all he was, or ever could be, was hers.

The soft fabric of his suit felt coarse against her sensitized hot skin, strangely wanton, her body totally naked and his fully clothed. His mouth adored her breast, teasing the dusky aureole until Edie whimpered with relief when he drew her into the heat of his mouth and then nuzzled the soft, tender flesh beneath. Daniel drew a moist half-circle with his tongue, and then again. Short feathery kisses followed the same pattern, and then over the gentle curve of her stomach, and she was dizzy with joy.

The soft rasp of her breath purled around them, and then Edie sighed, long and deep: his fingers found what they sought.

He caressed until she was swollen and pulsing with arousal, the tight nub bursting with passion. Edie's body jerked and, for an instant, he waited, hands stroking gently, relentlessly, until her low moan of pleasure reassured him. Daniel lowered his mouth and placed a long, tender kiss on the dusky triangle and his head was filled with the sweet, intimate perfume of her. His hand slid over the pulsing bud with gentle evocative thrusts until he felt the trembling spasms begin to shake her.

"Oh God, Daniel, I . . . I'm aching . . . please, I—I need you. Come to me, love, come inside me . . . now!"

"Ssh, sweetheart," he kissed her lightly, "yes . . . oh yes!"

Half mad with his own aroused desire, he hurriedly discarded his constricting clothing, never ceasing his fevered caresses. And then he was lying over her, his elbows on either side supporting him. Edie opened her arms and took him to her, savagely, possessively. They stared at each other for a breath, in a silent vow, her body moving against his rigid arousal. He pushed past the moist welcome of her passion into the hot velvet that quickly, tightly, sheathed his.

There was a bright explosion in her heart. Her body thrust up to meet him, an inexorable need to be closer, closer! Edie was impatient that even their skin should separate them. She arched as Daniel began to move inside her, gently at first, not allowing her to rush their pace. This was forever.

Her scent surrounded him, the heady redolence of jasmine and musk and passion. He buried his head between her breasts, inhaling the sweet perfume of her body, his breath hot on her skin. When he raised his head and took one nub into his mouth, then the other, his lips and tongue echoed with an agonizing languor the slow, steady rhythm of their bodies.

Their movements quickened and they began a dizzying climb, as if they would burst free of the familiar, the known, into a new dimension of experience, beyond this time and this place.

In the subdued light their eyes caught and held. At that moment when supreme fulfillment exploded within them they were looking at each other . . . watching the reflection of love.

Hours later, the faint sound of Jefferson Avenue's traffic drifting up through the windows, they lay huddled together in his massive bed, each holding the other with the possessiveness of a greedy child clutching his favorite teddy bear.

Daniel turned her face gently toward him, the haze of passion still shining in her amber eyes, a tender smile tucked into the corners of her lips. He smoothed the damp curls back from her forehead, then buried his face in her hair.

"Ah Edie, sweet, sweet Edie. How you've changed my world."

"Thank heaven you came after me tonight. I . . . God, Daniel, I was so ashamed, and afraid."

"Did you honestly think I would let you go like that? After the five weeks I've just been through?"

"I thought you'd never forgive me—"

"*Forgive* you? For what? Lorraine?" He grinned.

"Chalk that up to me—glad to take the credit. Thank God for Lorraine!"

As if to thank him for the compliment, a sad, basset hound face peered over the edge of the bed, her cool, soft nose tickling Edie's thigh.

"What—! Oh Lord, that's embarrassing. Like having an audience."

"She just wanted to be where the action was," he grinned. "Anyway, it's only Lorraine, not your mother."

Edie grinned, recalling the scene they'd left behind. "Not yours, either, thank heaven!"

He grimaced. "Did we have to bring *her* into our bedroom? Being in the same city is too close. And, let me assure you again, if you need it, tonight she asked for it, in spades! I almost let her have it myself, a couple of times. Frankly, until now, I didn't care enough to bother. Until tonight. Tonight I cared very much." He held her tighter and smiled. "Actually, I'm kind of glad I *didn't* do anything. I think you proved to yourself you can handle anything she can dish out. I seriously doubt you'll ever have to worry about being intimidated!" He paused deliberately and gazed into her eyes. "Everything you said tonight was perfect. And I do mean everything!"

"Which specific 'everything' do you mean?"

"Ohhh, no, no backing out now. I heard it from your own lips, with witnesses, and believe me," he laughed, "it'll be a long time before they forget *anything* said in that room tonight."

"What," she asked, puzzled, "are you talking about?"

"About us, about tomorrow—all our tomorrows. About forever. About love." His quiet, sure voice sent great shuddering waves of joy through her heart. She hadn't thought he'd notice the three small words, not among all those others!

"I never did ask, did I? But you'll have to marry

me. After all, you said you love me!" He stroked her hair. "Ah Edie, if I weren't such a blind fool I wouldn't have waited to hear it. I should have known— you've shown me in a hundred different ways, and I never gave you anything back." She would have protested but he kissed her quiet.

"The one thing I never learned was how to love. And I didn't even know I didn't know. Then you gave me a glimpse of what life could be, *should* be, and . . . I wanted it, God how I wanted it! How I wanted you!" Daniel kissed her forehead, her eyelids, and tasted the salt of her quiet tears of joy.

"Mmm, Edith Stephanie Calvin, I do love you." It was the first time he had ever uttered those words in his life. "I *love* you, you wonderful, crazy one-woman demolition derby, you! How could I not love someone who enjoys liver and onions, and who can't keep her hands off me? And with the dog thrown into the deal— an irresistible combination!"

"My mother didn't raise a stupid kid. . . . I'm not about to let you get away now that you've finally gotten around to asking."

They grinned at each other. "Oh, Daniel, I love you so very much! My God," she gave a mock shudder, "I *must*, to take another plunge into 'Lifestyles of the Rich and Sleazy'—present company, of course, excepted. That's the last thing in the world anyone could ever say about you. Make that 'the Rich and Stuffy.' "

"Well, we're not all stuffy, you know."

"Not anymore, *we're* not." She settled herself into the pillows, sighed. "At least I hope not. You know, I've never been crazy about life among the city dudes, but for you it's worth it. Oh yes, my darling Danny boy, it's worth it!"

His eyes filled and he hugged her tightly.

"And after all it won't be a problem professionally speaking—ah, dare I use the dreaded 'P' word?"

He groaned. "Damn, you don't forget anything, do you?"

"Nothing important." She held his face between her hands, love shining from her eyes. "Do you think you'll get tired of hearing me say 'I love you' so much?"

"Well, I might," he said softly, smoothing the tousled hair back from her temples, "in about forty or fifty years. Keep testing me, though, will you, just to make sure?" He kissed her then, a gentle and tender union that told her more about the depth of his love than anything he could have said.

For a few moments they lay together, Daniel cradling her in his arms. "Edie, there's something we have to talk about."

"Lord, you sound so serious. We're not back to stuffy so soon, are we?" she teased.

He touched her nose. "Don't get fresh. But it is serious. It's about us, our future." He felt her tense in his arms. "No, idiot, it's nothing like that. We're together, nothing will ever change that." His voice faded and he turned his head, staring out the window at the night sky.

"When I first came back from up north, I was angry, I mean *really* angry—at you, at myself, at the world— it was so unfair. That was the first stage, a good long dose of self-pity. I found I'm really good at it. Too good. You'll have to keep your foot ready to kick me in the ass when I start to relapse. You're so good at that!" She could hear the smile in his voice.

"Then, when I finally forced myself to take the first step, get back to my work, I kicked into the next level—fear. I was afraid. Hell, I was scared to death. I'd been fine when I was up north, but how would it be back here? Had anything changed, really? Had I changed?" He felt her weight shift, knew she was looking at him intently but he didn't look back.

"I learned a lot up in Pecomish Springs, about myself, about what life can offer, what life can be. And, you know, I found the void I'd always felt in my life wasn't lethal anymore." Daniel smiled and hugged her closer. "Just knowing there's an Edie Calvin somewhere in the world was enough to put some color into the gray life I've always lived. It wasn't good, but it was tolerable, and I'd learned I could live with it, if I had to."

"But you don't have to," Edie murmured.

"And I'll thank God for that every day of my life!" For a few seconds they held each other but Edie sensed he wasn't finished. Then he spoke.

"Funny, I just couldn't stop thinking about that little town, how much I missed it. And last night, when you marched in that door and back into my life, everything just sort of fell into place. Tell me, Edie, the truth: if you had your choice, would you rather live here," he gestured at the luxurious apartment, the view out the window, "or up in Pecomish Springs?"

It was the last thing Edie had expected him to say. She'd never hidden her distaste for living in the world he'd grown up in, but had she stressed it too much? Was he feeling guilty? Did he think it a major obstacle? If she denied it now, could they base their lives on that lie? Deception would be a flimsy base for a marriage and a life, they both knew it. He'd asked for truth— she could give him nothing less.

"I came back from Chicago for a temporary haven, to let my mother and that feeling of 'home' take the place of pain and anger and failure. I thought eventually I'd leave again, but I found I didn't *want* to leave. I know myself well enough to be sure I'm not a mama's girl; I just loved being back there, loved the people, the atmosphere, the quiet and simplicity. Life is complex enough, at least for me, and after a while I knew that was the place I truly wanted to be." She put her hand on his cheek. "Until you left. I learned something very important then, Daniel. Where you are is my place."

He suddenly found it hard to swallow. He blinked away those unfamiliar tears and kissed her again, hard and deep and sure. "Well, if I'm going to be stuck with you forever, it might as well be in a place I really like!" Edie's heart literally stopped for a moment, until he went on. "I know the hospital board needs someone to be head of surgery, and I can always lend a hand 'birthin' babies' with Doctor Dressler. I've got a house and a skating pond and it seems a shame to let them go to waste. So . . ." The sentence hung in the air between them, unfinished.

"You—you'd give up your practice, everything you have here—?

"I have nothing here, Edie, don't you know that? Not without you."

Abruptly she sat up beside him, hands clenched around the edge of the sheet and leaned over him. "But you do have me, no matter what. Oh, Daniel, please, don't do this for me. If you regret it someday, you'll regret *us*, and I couldn't bear that. We can have a wonderful life here, I *know* that; you don't have to move up north because you think it will make me happy. *You* make me happy, I don't need anything else."

He gazed up at her, smiled. "Yes, I know. And that's exactly why I know this is the right thing to do. Because of what we have, what we found up there, I was able to prove to myself that I could do what I had to do here. I was able to resume surgery, I had the confidence to make the necessary decisions, to take the responsibility for those life-and-death decisions. The headaches were gone, and I could take up the life I'd run away from. But now I know that I *can*, I also know I don't want to, and so I don't *have* to. Can you understand what I'm trying to say?"

Edie sucked in her breath, afraid to believe that life could be so perfect. "I think you were afraid you'd never see Sweet Lorraine again. She's the bait, right?"

"Actually," he laughed, dragging her down to his arms again, "it's a toss-up between her and your mother's cookies. If I have to take you in the bargain, well, I'll do my best to hold up under the strain."

"From past experience you 'hold up' very well!" she answered happily. "Why don't we make sure one more time?" She slid her hands down his chest, his stomach, and he laughed.

"My God, forget forty or fifty years . . . I hope I can last for the rest of the night!"

Edie smiled dreamily. "That sounds beautiful: forty or fifty years." She stopped suddenly, staring down at him. "But, Daniel! What about your patients here?"

"I told you once, no one's indispensable. *Except you!* And anyway, once I'm through with them, if I'm any good at all, they shouldn't need me much afterwards." He smiled at her. "I can always work out a schedule where I commute once a month or so, to do consultations, surgery, whatever. We'll see. After all I'm not going to the moon, just four hours away. I'm within reach if anyone thinks they need me."

Suddenly Edie grinned at him. "Your mother will be thrilled to hear all this. God, you'll be totally lost forever out in the wasteland of western Michigan, disreputable and unredeemable. Poor foolish Daniel! And that reminds me, you *really* don't care what a social dud I am?"

"Dud?" He laughed so long and hard the bed shook. "Honey, after tonight, any invitation we extend would be the hit of the social season—if Pecomish Springs has a social season, and if you really care. *I* sure as hell don't! I know that people down here would beg to come to a party with you, just to see who your sparring partner would be!"

She pinched him where it would hurt the most. "Smart mouth! The only *sparring* I want to do is right here in this bed with you."

"Well, yeah, I'll go along with that." He tightened his embrace and they held each other, radiant with happiness. Now no barriers remained, for either of them. They could face each other with no secrets, no fears, no memories to dim the incredible joy of their love.

Daniel pulled back for an instant. "Wait, there's just one more thing I have to do." He rose, stepped over the bulk of Lorraine's prostrate body, and walked to the dresser. Edie loved the un-self-conscious beauty of his body as he moved across the room. He rummaged in a drawer, found what he wanted, and pulled open another. Then she saw the surgical scissors in his hand and watched curiously as he proceeded to reduce the items in the drawer to precisely cut shreds of material.

"What *are* you doing, Daniel?" She gaped at him.

"Hey, what happened to 'Danny boy'?" His teasing smile was probably the most beautiful sight Edie had ever seen. He looked years younger without the burden of bitter loneliness he'd carried for so long.

"Just finishing what you started." He sifted his hand through the shredded fabric, the silky tatters clinging to his fingers. Then he held up what she now recognized as the remains of a pajama bottom. "I'm sure I'll have no use for these."

"How true, how true. Oh Danny boy, you've come a long way, baby." They grinned at each other, thinking of just how far he *had* come.

Daniel beckoned her to the sliding glass door and out to the broad terrace beyond. She shivered slightly as cold air and bare skin came together. With a grandly theatrical gesture he tossed the small heap of newly created rags up and out into the night sky. "And now we bid farewell to the old Daniel Slayton."

"Well, hello, Danny!"

He pulled Edie back into the circle of his arms, warming her with himself and his love, and the only shivers she felt were from his nearness, his lips pressed warmly to her temple, the strength of his sheltering embrace.

Neither felt the chill winter night as they turned to each other. "Well, I seem to have lost a lot of things since I met you," he smiled, his eyes filled with a tender light. "Pain, inhibitions, an entire wardrobe . . . and one damned heavy albatross!"

"Mmm," Edie purred, snuggling closer in his arms. "I *love* you uninhibited and naked!" Smiling, she stood on tiptoe and kissed him, then pulled him back into the room and slid the door closed just as something heavy and warm and furry brushed her leg. They looked down to see Lorraine settle her bulk across their feet, satisfied and content, as if she'd finally steered them to the course she'd envisaged all along.

They smiled fondly down at her for a moment, then looked out again through the glass and watched the last of the silken scraps float away aimlessly before the breeze. They resembled a flock of small birds, dipping and wheeling in the cold drafts of air . . . or, perhaps, a good-sized albatross, now taking wing forever.

THE BEGINNING

SHARE THE FUN . . .
SHARE YOUR NEW-FOUND TREASURE!!

You don't want to let your new books out of your sight?
That's okay. Your friends can get their own. Order below.

No. 151 DANIEL by Joan Shapiro
Daniel and Edie are destined for each other but they're a lethal combo!

No. 18 RAINBOW WISHES by Jacqueline Case
Mason is looking for more from life. Evie may be his pot of gold!

No. 19 SUNDAY DRIVER by Valerie Kane
Carrie breaks through all Cam's defenses showing him how to love.

No. 21 THAT JAMES BOY by Lois Faye Dyer
Jesse believes in love at first sight. Will he convince Sarah?

No. 22 NEVER LET GO by Laura Phillips
Ryan has a big dilemma. Kelly is the answer to *all* his prayers.

No. 23 A PERFECT MATCH by Susan Combs
Ross can keep Emily safe but can he save himself from Emily?

No. 24 REMEMBER MY LOVE by Pamela Macaluso
Will Max ever remember the special love he and Deanna shared?

No. 25 LOVE WITH INTEREST by Darcy Rice
Stephanie & Elliot find $47,000,000 *plus* interest—true love!

No. 26 NEVER A BRIDE by Leanne Banks
The last thing Cassie wanted was a relationship. Joshua had other ideas.

No. 27 GOLDILOCKS by Judy Christenberry
David and Susan join forces and get tangled in their own web.

No. 28 SEASON OF THE HEART by Ann Hammond
Can Lane and Maggie's newfound feelings stand the test of time?

No. 31 WINGS OF LOVE by Linda Windsor
Mac & Kelly soar to new heights of ecstasy. Are they ready?

No. 32 SWEET LAND OF LIBERTY by Ellen Kelly
Brock has a secret and Liberty's freedom could be in serious jeopardy!

No. 33 A TOUCH OF LOVE by Patricia Hagan
Kelly seeks peace and quiet and finds paradise in Mike's arms.

No. 34 NO EASY TASK by Chloe Summers
Hunter is wary when Doone delivers a package that will change his life.

No. 35 DIAMOND ON ICE by Lacey Dancer
Diana could melt even the coldest of hearts. Jason hasn't a chance.

No. 36 DADDY'S GIRL by Janice Kaiser
Slade wants more than Andrea is willing to give. Who wins?

No. 37 ROSES by Caitlin Randall
It's an inside job & K.C. helps Brett find more than the thief!

No. 38 HEARTS COLLIDE by Ann Patrick
Matthew finds big trouble and it's spelled P-a-u-l-a.

No. 40 CATCH A RISING STAR by Laura Phillips
Justin is seeking fame; Beth helps him find something more important.

No. 41 SPIDER'S WEB by Allie Jordan
Silvia's quiet life explodes when Fletcher shows up on her doorstep.

No. 43 DUET by Patricia Collinge
Adam & Marina fit together like two perfect parts of a puzzle!

No. 44 DEADLY COINCIDENCE by Denise Richards
J.D.'s instincts tell him he's not wrong; Laurie's heart says trust him.

No. 46 ONE ON ONE by JoAnn Barbour
Vincent's no saint but Loie's attracted to the devil in him anyway.

Meteor Publishing Corporation
Dept. 693, P. O. Box 41820, Philadelphia, PA 19101-9828

Please send the books I've indicated below. Check or money order (U.S. Dollars only)—no cash, stamps or C.O.D.s (PA residents, add 6% sales tax). I am enclosing $2.95 plus 75¢ handling fee for *each* book ordered.

Total Amount Enclosed: $_____.

____ No. 151	____ No. 24	____ No. 32	____ No. 38
____ No. 18	____ No. 25	____ No. 33	____ No. 40
____ No. 19	____ No. 26	____ No. 34	____ No. 41
____ No. 21	____ No. 27	____ No. 35	____ No. 43
____ No. 22	____ No. 28	____ No. 36	____ No. 44
____ No. 23	____ No. 31	____ No. 37	____ No. 46

Please Print:
Name _____

Address _____ Apt. No. _____

City/State _____ Zip _____

Allow four to six weeks for delivery. Quantities limited.